ALSO BY

Stand Alone Romances:

The Fall in Love Checklist

Hero Ever After

Soul Mates in Romeo Romance Series:

Chasing Romeo

Love Not at First Sight

Romance by the Book

Find these books and more by Sarah Ready at:

www.sarahready.com/romance-books

Sign up to receive bonus content, exclusive epilogues and more at:
www.sarahready.com/newsletter

WHEN ROMANCE DOESN'T GO BY THE BOOK...

Book-loving librarian Jessie has loved Gavin Williams for practically her whole life. So when a psychic predicts that Gavin is Jessie's one fated soul mate, she's ecstatic.

There's just one *itty bitty* little problem.

Gavin's engaged to marry another woman.

What's a book lover to do? Easy. Check out dozens of romance books, study the (totally realistic) way characters fall in love, and make a foolproof plan on how to win her soul mate (in one week).

Meet cute? Check.

Dance under the stars? Check.

Kiss in the rain? Check.

Romance books don't lie – it'll all go perfectly.

Except, there's *another* problem. Gavin's twin brother: William Williams IV.

Jessie has hated William for as long as she's loved his brother. William is grump to Jessie's sunshine, stand-offish to her extrovert, cold to her warm. And when William learns of

Jessie's plan to derail his brother's engagement he swears that he'll do anything to stop her.

But after William and Jessie (unwillingly) share a dance...a romantic dinner...a kiss...Jessie starts to wonder, is *William* actually her soul mate? Or is this just another one of his games?

She can't tell, because this romance definitely isn't going by the book.

romance by the book

SARAH READY

CROWN

W.W. CROWN BOOKS
An imprint of Swift & Lewis Publishing LLC
www.wwcrown.com

Library of Congress Control Number: 2021914217
ISBN: 978-1-954007-15-4 (eBook)
ISBN: 978-1-954007-16-1 (pbk)
ISBN: 978-1-954007-17-8 (large print)

romance by the book

1

JESSIE

I FELL in love when I was eight years old, and it was the best and the worst day of my life. My mom always said, in a town like Romeo, you're guaranteed to find your true love, it's not a matter of if, only of when. For me, the when happened early.

Some (okay, everyone) might say I live in a fantasy world, that no one can find their soul mate when they're eight years old. But I did. And Miss Erma is about to confirm it.

That's right. Romeo, New York's number one star, Miss Erma, official soul mate psychic, finally saw my true love.

I always promised myself that if Miss Erma ever predicted my soul mate, I'd pursue him with a single-minded passion. I'd do anything for that kind of love. Romeo, the town where I grew up, inspires this kind of thinking. We have more happily matched couples and true love than any other town in the Western Hemisphere. Our small town has a Cupid festival, a Valentine's Day parade, a Sweetheart's Day baking contest, and a 30, 40, or 50 year wedding anniversary practically every week. If the cobblestone streets, the overflowing flower baskets, and the cute stone bridge over the river doesn't convince you, then our charm will—Romeo, Official Town of Love USA, is the place where true love finds you.

Needless to say, I've been dreaming of this moment for practically my whole life.

"You've seen him?" I ask Miss Erma.

She gives me a smile that on anyone below twenty I'd call mischievous, but Miss Erma is over eighty, so I'll call it conspiratorial. "I have," she confirms. "I saw him this morning."

My stomach does a flip and I clasp my hands together to keep from jumping up and down and shouting in glee. We're in a library after all. Miss Erma is here for the class I teach, a seniors' computer skills class. There's no jumping around or shouting in libraries.

But still. This, this is the moment I've been waiting for.

Miss Erma told my friends Chloe and Veronica their soul mates in the last year, and I just knew my time would be coming soon. Well, if not *knew*, then hoped.

Miss Erma adjusts her silk shawl over her shoulders. It has pink cherry blossoms on ivory colored fabric. Then she leans back in her computer chair and beams at me.

"I've finished the internet search assignment. I looked up travel plans for New York City. Wanda and I are planning a trip," says Erma.

What? This is the most important moment of my life and she wants to talk about the computer class assignment? I look around the library community room. It's a big, bright room, with a long table filled with computers and comfy desk chairs. The walls are painted cream and the carpet is sage green. Everyone in the class is still at work, ignoring my conversation with Erma.

"Miss Erma, please. My soul mate. Who is he?" I ask, and then I hold my breath.

But a horrifying thought enters my mind. What if she says William?

No.

Please not William. Please not William. Please not William.

Please don't say William Williams IV.

Please not—

"It's that Williams boy."

The breath I was holding shoots out in a loud exhale. I cough and hit my chest.

Wanda, Erma's best friend, looks over from her computer. "Are you alright, dear?"

"Fine. Fine." I wave at her.

Everyone else in the class is absorbed in their internet search assignment. They haven't noticed Erma and me talking.

I cough again and clear my throat. My stomach feels like it's on a roller coaster, it's being tossed around and I can't get off the ride.

"The Williams boy?" I ask.

Please be Gavin. Please be Gavin. Please be the boy I've wanted since I was eight years old, not his awful, horrible brother.

"That's right," says Erma. She winks at me and then digs around in her purse. It's on the floor next to her chair. When she comes up she's holding a cookie tin. She opens it and holds it in front of me. "Have an oatmeal raisin cookie. I baked them this morning."

I look down at the pile of cookies in the red tin. How can Erma offer cookies at a time like this? My stomach is still looping around my abdomen. Doesn't she realize there are two Williams boys? One is perfect and wonderful and everything I've ever wanted and the other is...Will.

She waves the tin under my nose, and the scent of cinnamon and raisins wafts up to me.

"Um, alright. Thank you." I take a cookie chock-full of raisins from the top of the pile, then I force myself to take a bite, chew and swallow. "Mmm. Really good. Thank you."

I set the cookie down on the table, there's no way I'll be able to force myself to swallow another bite. Not until I know. Is my soul mate the man I've always believed it was, or his awful, horrible, rotten brother.

"Miss Erma? Which Williams boy? There are two of them."

"Hmm. Are there?"

She puts the lid back on the cookie tin and pops it into her purse. When she comes back up, her black hair is messy. She pats it down and re-straightens her shawl. She's fine boned and petite, and some people say she looks like a little bird. She definitely has the energy of a bird. And I'm beginning to see why Chloe always insists her great aunt is full of mischief.

"Yes. There's Gavin and there's William."

My stomach rolls again and I press my hand against it. Please don't say William, please don't say William. She couldn't, she wouldn't.

"He just came back to town," she says.

"Yes. Which one? Which one is my soul mate?"

Miss Erma studies me as if I'm missing the point. She gives me the same look that Chloe gives me when I can't visualize one of her greeting card illustration ideas. I'd laugh if I weren't so frustrated.

"Jessie. Dear. You already know who your soul mate is."

"I do?" I try to swallow down the dry cookie crumbs still sticking in my throat. "Does that mean...?"

Miss Erma nods. "Your soul mate is the Williams boy you've loved since you were a little girl."

Not William Williams IV. Not Will.

Thank you, God. Thank you.

It's Gavin. His twin.

4

"He's my soul mate," I say with wonder.

Erma's eyes twinkle. "That's right. You've known he was for years."

I grab Erma's hands in mine and then I start jumping up and down and squealing. I can't help it. This is the best day of my life.

Miss Erma laughs and shakes her head. She's probably used to this reaction. But me, this is my one and only time to learn the name of my soul mate, and it's Gavin.

"What is it? What's happened?" asks Wanda.

She hurries over. But I can't answer, I'm too busy spinning in a circle. I feel like Maria in *The Sound of Music*. Any minute, I'm going to stop spinning and start singing to the mountains.

I've been transported to my own personal heaven. It's finally happened.

After six years, Gavin Williams is finally back in Romeo, and according to Erma, he's mine.

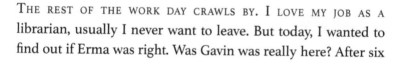

THE REST OF THE WORK DAY CRAWLS BY. I LOVE MY JOB AS A librarian, usually I never want to leave. But today, I wanted to find out if Erma was right. Was Gavin was really here? After six years of absence, was he back?

Finally I leave work. I speed across town and park on the side of the road next to a five-acre field full of tall grass, chicory flowers, Queen Anne's lace, and milkweed. One of the Williams' summer houses is on the other side of the field. I pull a pair of binoculars out of the glove box. Veronica, one of my friends, gave them to me for Christmas a few years ago as a man-watching joke. I never thought they'd actually come in handy. I tilt the rear-view mirror my way. Put on lipstick, finger brush my permanently frizzy hair, smooth my wrinkled dress —1950s vintage as usual—and rush out of the car.

I run across the field. The smell of sweet grass rises and reminds me of childhood and hugs from my mom. I reach the old oak and press my hand against its deeply grooved bark. I take a moment to catch my breath. An ant crawls across my hand and I flick it off. When my heart stops beating so hard, I kick off my saddle shoes and tights. It's been a long time, but I always climbed this tree best barefoot.

I look over my shoulder at the Williams house and a smile, bigger than I've had in years, spreads across my face. The sun comes out from behind the clouds and shines on the house. I take it as another sign. I finally, finally will be loved again.

I hoist myself up onto the first limb and climb a long-ago-memorized path up to a sturdy branch for the perfect view. I position my hunter green stretch twill dress over my legs and settle in. I pull the lens cap off the binoculars and point them at Gavin's window.

If Erma's right and he's back...

Then...

"What are you doing in my tree?"

I startle and drop the binoculars. The strap catches them and they thud against my chest. My heart pounds.

Gavin.

I look down at the man and catch my breath.

Even from fifteen feet away his blue eyes hold me in place. For a moment, I can't move. I don't remember there being this much awareness between us, or of him having this much command in the way he stands.

I want to agree. This is his tree, his field, his world, and I'm his too. I can almost touch the pull between us, the need and connection is so strong.

"Gavin." My voice comes out husky and hopeful.

His head snaps back. His demeanor shifts, it was open before, now it's glacial cold. His hooded eyes narrow on me, and even though I'm fifteen feet above him, it feels like he's looking down on me.

Oh no.

Oh, no no no.

He's not Gavin.

I can tell from the expression on his face. He has that sort of permanently superior, elevated-above-humanity, never-made-a-mistake-in-his-life expression that grates on me.

"Hello, William. Long time no see." I swallow my embarrassment at my inappropriate reaction to him. He's not Gavin.

"Jessie," he acknowledges. Then, "Why are you in my tree?" His voice is colder than before.

"It's not your tree. Besides, I'm birdwatching. Your property ends two feet behind you." I point to a patch of blue chicory flowers in the field behind him.

He doesn't turn around to look. He just folds his arms across his chest and lifts an eyebrow.

Years ago, I tried to be his friend, but I quickly learned William Williams IV doesn't need friends. He just needs a checkbook, a ledger, and a business. Even at fifteen he was a cold, arrogant robot.

"Anyway..." I say, hoping he leaves.

"Are you aware, being a peeping Tom is a criminal offense?"

My cheeks flush. "I'm not! I can't even see anything."

A satisfied smile spreads over his face and I realize I practically admitted to what I'm doing. I look at his expensive captain-of-industry suit and wonder how I mistook him for Gavin.

Will grabs the lowest branch on the tree and boosts himself up. I gasp as the tree shakes.

"What are you doing?" I squeak.

The branches are thick and sturdy and beautifully spaced for climbing. William, six foot three, muscular and fit, has no trouble climbing up, even in a suit.

I'm sitting on a limb perfectly positioned to see into the wide windows of the Williams' mansion.

Yes...to my everlasting shame, I spent many nights as a 14-year-old watching Gavin make out with his multitude of girlfriends. I dreamed of the day I'd be in his house and not this tree. I imagined it down to what I'd wear, what he'd say, then I'd make out with the back of my hand and finally descend into a fit of laughter.

But, 14 years later, I'm still in the tree. William is still laughing at me. And Gavin doesn't know I exist.

William manages to lift himself onto the branch next to me. The limb which I previously thought of as sturdy and wide suddenly feels too small and precarious. I grab at the bark and dig my fingers in.

Will relaxes, loose limbed and comfortable in the tree. His eyes glint and he smirks as he looks down at my white-knuckled hand.

"Jessie." He tilts his head in greeting.

A lock of sandy brown hair falls over his eyes and I watch as he brushes it aside.

"Will," I say in a choked voice. Why does he have to look just like Gavin? It messes with my head. I can tell them apart from the way they stand, or talk, or heck, look at me. But I still feel a traitorous flip in my stomach around Will.

It's been six weeks since Will was last in Romeo, but it's been six years since Gavin's been here. I wonder if his hair is shorter than Will's? I wonder if when he sees me he'll feel a spark?

Now that Erma has seen us together, I'm sure he will.

When Erma told me he was in town, I had to see for myself. I had to know. Hence, the childhood oak tree of shame.

Will leans over and reaches for me. I gasp as his hands brush my dress and he slowly lifts the binoculars strap over my head. I hold still because I'm scared of making any sudden moves. I lick my lips and he smirks. I wonder if he's remembering the time we kissed in this tree? By the smirk, I'd guess yes.

The jerk.

"Those are mine," I finally say, pointing to the binoculars.

Will lifts his eyebrow and shrugs. Then he looks through the binoculars. He fiddles with the focus and the magnification. As he does, my cheeks start to burn. I know what he'll find. Finally, his shoulders stiffen and I know when he sees exactly what I was looking at.

Slowly he lowers the binoculars, then hands them back to me. They land hot and heavy in my palm. I turn away although I can feel Will studying my face.

The humid evening air presses on me and I can't quite pull in a full breath. I squirm on the branch and the scratchy bark irritates my skin. It's as if he can see everything I try to hide, all my fears, all my hopes, my dreams. A drop of sweat trickles down my chest.

"I didn't..." I say, but then trail off.

Because I think I see disappointment in his expression. Now, there's been a lot of emotions between us in the past twenty years—antagonism, indifference, straight-up dislike, but never disappointment.

"He's getting married," says Will.

The sheen of sweat turns cold and my stomach drops. "What?" It comes out like a croak. That's not possible. "He can't."

Will narrows his eyes. They go ice cold and not even the lines around them can soften his expression. "He can. He is."

"He can't..."

It can't be.

Erma just confirmed Gavin is my soul mate, something I've dreamed of nearly my entire life. She told me Gavin was back in Romeo. It was like everything was finally, finally falling into place. William's words crash over me like a bucket of ice. My soul mate is marrying another woman?

"Of course he can," says Will. "He's here for a week; his engagement party is Saturday. Then he's getting married."

Will moves to climb down from the tree, then pauses. I look at him, taking in his features. Sure, he's Gavin's identical twin, but I always wondered how two people who look so much alike could be so completely different.

Will has ice-blue eyes. Gavin, a happy blue. Will has a hard chin, a hooked nose and a full lower lip. On Gavin, that lower lip looks mischievous and inviting. On Will, it looks...wicked. The one soft part on a hard uncompromising man. Taste it and maybe it will unlock the rest of him.

"Look," he says.

I look into his eyes. I can tell he's about to say something I won't like.

"I know you've always had this unrealistic little-girl crush on my brother—"

I blink. "That's not true."

He pointedly looks down at the binoculars and then back up at me.

I flush.

He continues and his voice isn't gentle. "It's time to come back to reality. And it looks like I'm the one who has to help you do it."

"Not necessary," I say. In fact, Will is going to feel like a fool when I marry his brother. My embarrassment shifts to anger. My love life is none of Will's business.

Will sighs and points at the Williams' house. It's a stately, white-columned, colonial revival mansion from the 1920s. Three stories, eight bedrooms, four bathrooms, a grand staircase, a formal dining room, a conservatory, and a landscaped backyard that once hosted some of the most beautiful summer parties for the New York City elite.

"See that house?" he asks.

I nod. Of course I see it. That house featured a starring role in many of my childhood dreams.

Then Will turns and points in the opposite direction back toward the house where I grew up. It's an old single-wide trailer from the 1970s. Faded blue and rust-stained white siding, cement blocks for stairs, dingy princess sheets for curtains.

"See that house?" he asks.

I don't need to turn to know what it looks like.

"Yes."

A thick lump lodges in my throat. I see where he's going with this. Will has never sugarcoated his opinions.

"You and my brother are as different as those two houses. Even if he weren't getting married, which he is, the two of you would never work. No matter how much you wish you were, you will never be the type of woman Gavin wants. I guarantee it." He says this with so much certainty that I remember why I dislike him. Why I've always disliked him. He may be a financial genius, and he may have single-handedly saved his family's business from bankruptcy at age 14, and he may have the business world at his feet, but...he has no heart, no capability to love.

His closed off expression, his awful words, and the news that Gavin is marrying hit me again and I blink back tears. I look at his pressed suit and his cold face and I do what my mom always warned me against. I speak before thinking.

"I feel sorry for you."

"Really?" he drawls.

"Really. You don't know anything about love. About what someone will do or give. I think when you and your brother were born, he got a heart and you got a calculator. Maybe you can't see anybody loving me because you just see me as a poor investment, but not everybody sees people as numbers. So yeah, I feel sorry for you. Because with a calculator for a heart and a ledger for a soul you're never going to find love. Never."

I stop, and as soon as I do, remorse floods me. Will blinks and a small line forms between his brows.

He nods and swallows. "Right. Glad we set things straight. Stay clear of Gavin. He doesn't need your crush as a distraction."

I shake my head then grab the branch and drop down to the next lowest limb.

"Bye, Will."

I slide down the tree and drop to the ground. The binoculars knock against my chest. I grab my shoes and tights and hurry across the field back to the road. I don't look back, but I swear I can feel Will's gaze on me the whole while I'm walking away and long after he's out of sight.

It doesn't matter what Will says, there's nothing he can do to stop me from loving Gavin.

2

JESSIE

I DROP a two-foot-high stack of romance books and old romcoms from the library onto the thick wooden table top.

"Oh no, she's finally going off the deep end," says Veronica.

It's Monday, and I'm meeting my friends at Juliet's Wine Bar for our weekly girls night out. They're at our usual table, a scarred oak plank piece with comfy upholstered chairs and votive candles. The wine bar is crowded and the hum of happy conversation and laughter fills the air.

Veronica and Chloe already have some red wine poured from a bottle and Ferran has a bubbly white. There's a tray of cheese, crackers, and fruit. I pull out a chair and plop down. Ferran grabs an empty glass and pours me some of the red wine.

I grin at Veronica. She's the least romantic person I know. When Miss Erma told her the name of her soul mate, she ran. We may disagree on the importance of romance and romcoms, but I still love her.

"You won't believe what happened today." I smile at my best friends and gesture at the stack of books on the table.

"You got rid of the damaged books and nabbed enough goodies for a weeklong romance binge?" asks Ferran.

"Shoot me, shoot me now," Veronica says.

"Hey, you got *It Happened One Night*. Nick hasn't seen that yet." Chloe eyes the titles on the sack. "We watch movies after the baby's asleep and then reenact the sexy scenes. We did *Ghost* last week. I had no idea clay was so hard to get out of—"

"Um." A flush spreads over my cheeks at the visual.

"Have you done a *Spiderman* reenactment yet, that upside-down kiss?" asks Ferran.

"How do you think Nick got that sprained ankle last month?"

Veronica snorts and chokes on her wine. I pat her back.

Chloe winks. "Kidding. Just kidding."

"She's not," Ferran says in a loud whisper.

Veronica wipes her eyes. "I love you, Chloe. We should do a new card line—kinky stick figures doing it."

Chloe shakes her head and rolls her eyes.

I can't stand it anymore.

"You guys," I say. I wait until they're all looking. "I saw Miss Erma today." I put a whole book's worth of meaning into those five words.

Chloe's eyes widen. Erma is her great aunt and Chloe spent her life eating up Erma's romantic legacy.

"That's amazing," Chloe says. Her eyes light up. There's nothing Chloe loves more than romance. "Who is he? Where is he? What did she say?"

"Erma told you who your soul mate is?" Veronica asks.

I nod. Suddenly, I'm nervous. Maybe it's the way Veronica's looking at me. She spent years running from love and she wasn't excited when Erma told her who her soul mate was.

I turn and look at Ferran. She has a tight smile on her face.

Everyone knows Ferran loves her job more than anything in the world. She wouldn't be happy to have Erma's "help."

"Who is it?" asks Veronica.

I clear my throat and shove down my sudden nervousness.

"Gavin Williams."

There's a short silence, then Chloe says, "Isn't he...your first crush?"

More than crush. He's the one I've loved my whole life.

"That's him," I say.

"You used to write J.D. plus G.W. on all your school book covers. For years," Ferran says.

"Wow," Chloe says.

Ferran nods. "Wow. For once, Erma actually predicted a match that somebody's happy about."

Veronica shakes her head. "Gavin Williams is a player. That guy deflowered half of New York State's virgins while still in high school."

We all look at Veronica. She shrugs, and we burst out laughing. Veronica's husband was formerly The King of Players.

"He's a good man," I say with conviction. "I'm sure of it."

I think back to the day we met.

I'd just turned eight. I was wearing a scratchy black dress and itchy black tights. My grandma had pulled my hair into a tight French braid that made my eyes water. My mom was in a white lace dress, and her hair was smooth around her face, more silky and straight than it'd ever been when she was alive. Her skin was the wrong color and her lips were bright pink. Her coffin was pink too. And it made me angry and itchy because my mom hated pink. Hated it. But grandma said Dead People didn't care what color their coffin was. She told me to sit down, be quiet and shut up. My dad didn't say anything at all. He hadn't said anything for nearly a week.

When Grandma came, she saw that I hadn't eaten, or had a bath, or put on clean clothes for days.

Not since Mom died.

I'd been eating from the jar of pickles in the fridge. It was the only food left. Grandma took me to the bakery, bought me a ham sandwich and a glass of milk, and then back at home she screamed Dad back to life. After Mom's funeral and after Grandma left, Dad still didn't talk, but he never left the fridge empty again.

But that day, as I sat on the hard church pew in a scratchy dress, with an aching head, I kept quiet and I kept still and no matter how bad I wanted to cry and itch and let loose my hair and throw off my dress and tell everyone that the dead woman in the coffin wasn't my mom because my mom had curly hair, not smooth hair and my mom had pink cheeks, not orange-beige cheeks, I didn't. I kept quiet. I kept still. I imagined that somehow my mom wasn't really dead. That somehow she was still there, I just couldn't see her anymore.

When my dad and the others carried the pink coffin out, I ran from the church. I kicked off the shoes and the tights. I yanked out my braids. I tore off the itchy black dress so I was only in my cotton petticoat.

I ran and ran and ran. Until I ended up back home. But instead of going inside, I ran to the field. My chest ached and my legs were burning and itching from the run and my eyes stung from the sweat dripping.

I wiped at my eyes and sniffed.

"You're ugly."

I whipped my head up. There was a boy standing less than 10 feet away. He was my age and had on a formal navy blue school uniform.

I looked down at myself. My skin was blotchy and red, and my petticoat was old and dingy brown instead of white.

"I'm not," I said. My mom had always said I looked like her and my mom was beautiful.

"You are." Then the boy ran at me, an angry expression on his face. I stood still. Frozen by the snarl on his lips.

His hands hit my chest and he shoved me. Hard.

I flew back, my arms pinwheeling, and I hit the ground. I landed in the wet mud of the spongey springtime earth. The cold mud soaked through my petticoat and coated my legs and back. I tried to drag in a breath but I couldn't. The whole world was spinning and roaring. The boy came and stood over me.

"Told you so," he said.

Finally I pulled in a breath. Then I pushed it back out. He shrugged and walked away. I lay in the mud until the cold made my toes and fingers numb. When I sat up there was another boy there.

He looked the same as the last boy, except he had longer, shaggy hair and was wearing muddy jeans and a T-shirt.

"What're you doing?" he asked.

He cocked his head to the side and studied me. He didn't seem mean like the last boy, so I stood up and shrugged.

"Are you a twin?"

"Yes," he said defiantly. Then, "Wanna climb that tree with me?"

I looked at the big towering tree but didn't say anything. The boy gave me a half-smile, uncertain but friendly. Then he jogged to the tree and scrambled up.

I watched as his feet dangled from a limb and he kicked his legs back and forth.

"Come on," he shouted.

Suddenly, there was nothing I wanted more than to climb into the tall tree and leave the world behind. If I were high up, I'd be closer to my mom. I was the clumsiest climber, and by the time I reached the boy I was scratched and bleeding. He didn't mind. He grinned at me.

"You did it," he said. "We should be friends."

I looked at his soft smile, one front tooth missing, his shaggy, wild hair, and his bright blue eyes and I started to cry. I sniffed and used the back of my mud-caked arm to wipe my eyes.

The boy squirmed next to me and dug in his pocket. He pulled out a piece of string, a marble, a toy car, and finally a small navy blue hanky.

"Here. Sorry it's dirty. I used it to hold a field mouse this morning. I named her Mimi."

I took the handkerchief and wiped my eyes like a lady in an old movie.

"My mom died," I said. I don't know why I told him. I turned and looked through the leaves across the field.

"My mom left," he said finally. "She left last month. My dad says it's because she didn't love us."

"My mom loved me," I said.

He nodded solemnly. Then he took my hand and held it. I watched the breeze blow the bright green spring leaves and then I watched the high clouds speed by.

Finally he turned to me and said, "We can be friends if you want. Since both our moms are gone, we can take care of each other."

"Okay," I whispered.

Then I scrambled down from the tree. He followed, hopping down to the grass next to me. I bent down and snapped the stem of a bright blue chicory flower.

"Here," I held it out to him. "Friends."

He took it and we stood still. I felt something shift inside me, and although the horrible grief was still there, a small space had opened to let in hope. He did that for me. And that's when I knew. I loved him.

"Gavin," I heard a man yell.

The boy whipped his head around.

"I have to go," he said. "Bye."

He started to run, then stopped. "What's your name?" he called.

"Jessie. I live there." I pointed out the trailer across the field.

He grinned, waved the flower, and sprinted away toward huge mansion.

"Gavin," I whispered to myself. "Gavin." The name was a ray of hope on my lips.

He didn't come back.

Not the next day, not the next week, not for four years. And when Gavin did come back, he didn't seem to remember me at all. He was wild and fun. A bright light that danced into Romeo for a week or two every few years. I loved those weeks. Seeing him always reminded me of hope and friendship and having someone there even on the worst day of your life.

I pick up my wine glass and raise it in the air.

"I'd like to give a toast."

Veronica, Chloe and Ferran raise their glasses.

"To finding soul mates, to true love, and to friendship."

"To friendship," says Ferran.

"And soul mates," says Chloe.

"To true love," says Veronica.

We clink glasses and I swallow the local red wine. It has a bright berry flavor that I like.

Ferran clears her throat. "So, correct me if I'm wrong, but you haven't interacted with him since you were fourteen, right?"

"You're not wrong."

I served him a heart sugar cookie that said "Be Mine" at the Sweetheart's Day baking contest. He told me it was the best cookie he'd ever had. I blushed and stuttered and he sauntered away.

"So how do you know you actually should be with him?" asks Ferran.

"What?"

She shrugs and plays with the stem of her wineglass. "I know I'm the outlier here, but I think you should be careful or you'll end up choosing the wrong guy and the wrong life because someone else told you it was what you wanted and you listened when you should've questioned."

I sit still, stunned by what she's saying. I love my life, my job, and even before Erma confirmed it, I loved Gavin.

"I've known since I was a kid. And now Miss Erma has seen it. You should be happy for me."

Ferran grimaces. "Sorry, Jess. I'm just worried about you. Sometimes when you have an objective you get blinders."

I cross my arms over my chest, uncomfortable with what she's saying. Then I admit it. "You're right."

Veronica smiles. "Like that time she organized the book drive to raise money for the senior citizen zipline trip and all the seniors hated the idea of a zipline, but she wouldn't listen?"

I groan. That *was* a terrible idea. In my defense, I meant well.

"Or that time," says Chloe, "when she tried for weeks to start a cat-walking business in high school and she wouldn't listen when we told her a dog-walking business would work better."

I laugh. "Fine. Yes. I have flaws."

"We have many examples," says Veronica. "Don't make me bring up the tsunami preparedness and hurricane drills."

They all laugh and I roll my eyes. We live in upstate New York, far, far from the ocean. "I was 10."

"Still should've known better," says Ferran.

I fill my glass and signal Juliet for another bottle.

"Putting the past behind us, let's presume Miss Erma is right, because she's always right, and let's presume my twenty years of feelings for Gavin are also right, and let's form a plan."

"What kind of plan?" Chloe asks.

I point to the stack of books. "I have a week to get Gavin to notice me and fall in love with me. I'm going to use the guru tips of romantic literature and cinema to make it happen."

"You've lost your mind," Veronica says.

"No, it's a good idea," I argue. "For example, what does every romance have that jumpstarts the chemistry?"

"A sexy male lead?" asks Veronica.

"A meet-cute," Chloe says.

"Right! A clumsy heroine who literally falls into the hero's arms. I'm going to orchestrate a meet-cute."

"Oh no. This won't end well," Veronica says.

But Chloe and Ferran are into it. A full bottle of wine later, we've scoured plots, meet-cutes, romantic scenes, declarations of love, and all the ways book and movie characters fall in love and we have our list.

"Okay, here it is," I say.

I hold up my phone and glance at my notes screen.

"Everything I need to do for Gavin to realize I'm his one true love and then live happily ever after is right here. First step, the meet-cute."

"It's never going to work," Veronica says.

"Of course it will. It's meant to be. Nothing and no one can stop true love."

3

WILL

"I'M CALLING OFF THE WEDDING," Gavin says.

It takes a second for his words to sink in. When they do, a slight pinch of panic begins. I take a deep breath and look up from my desk at my twin brother.

He leans against the doorframe of my office. It's on the fourth floor and takes up the entire converted attic space in the old Romeo house. The walls are light blue, the floors wide oak plank, and the windows look over the grassy field, the old oak tree, and the country road that leads to town. I have a large desk, a desk chair, and a couch that I sleep on when I'm deep in work and want a few minutes' rest in the middle the night before starting up again. The rest of the space is empty. I had all the boxes and old furniture cleared out and donated when I converted the space to an office.

"You're calling off your wedding?" I ask in a calm voice, which is hard because I'd like to knock Gavin's head against the wall.

Gavin sighs, pushes off the doorframe and walks into the room.

"Yes," he says. He paces back and forth and clenches and unclenches his hands.

I stand up and walk out from behind the desk.

"No," I say.

Gavin stops pacing. He looks at me and shakes his head. His eyes are bloodshot and have bags under them. His clothes are rumpled.

"Excuse me?"

I roll my shoulders. "No. You aren't calling off the wedding."

"Dang it, Will—"

"Also, welcome back to good ol' Romeo. You look like hell. How was your flight?"

Gavin scowls at me. "It was crap. Do you know how much I hate flying from Bali to New York on short notice? There I was, on this sweet little catamaran...dang it Will, I'm calling it off."

I study my brother. We're identical twins, but nearly thirty years of living completely different lives has made noticeable differences in our appearances. Where I'm pale from living at the office and bulky from letting out stress at the gym, Gavin is more wiry and bronzed and has lines around his eyes from a decade of pursuing every outdoor activity on the planet. Scuba diving in the most exotic places in the world. Hang gliding in Rio de Janeiro. White-water rafting in forgotten rapids, which is how he met his fiancée, Lacey Duporte. She treated the snake bite he got while camping alongside a river in Cambodia.

Lacey saved Gavin's life. When he called me on the satellite phone, feverish and only half-lucid, he told me it was love at first sight and he was going to marry the woman who sucked snake venom from his leg. Turned out, Lacey was Dr. Lacey Duporte, an ER physician on a Doctors Without Borders trip. She lived in New York City and was close to her family.

The keywords here are "family" and "Duporte." Her father is Alan Duporte, owner and CEO of our largest competitor and our pending acquisition. The business deal hinges on Lacey and Gavin's wedding.

"Let's have a coffee." I take the back stairs down two at a time to the first floor. They're the old narrow servant stairs that lots of old mansions have. They're also the most convenient way to get to the kitchen from anywhere else in the house.

I start the industrial machine and make two espressos. Gavin tips both of them back, so I make another two. When it seems like the frantic, hunted look has somewhat left his eyes, I lean back against the cold marble counter and take a sip of the hot black espresso.

"So, why do you want to ruin your life and our family business by doing a stupid thing like calling off your wedding?"

Gavin closes his eyes and rubs his temples.

"I can't do it. She keeps asking me what color bedsheets I want, and what pattern of china, and if I want bath towels made in Turkey or Egypt." He looks up and his eyes are wide and desperate again. "I don't care where the damn towels are made. But she does. She does."

"Okay? And?"

He starts to pace the length of the kitchen, then stops.

"She wants a family, Will, and a home."

I nod. "That happens sometimes when you get married."

"I don't want a family." He smacks his hand against the marble counter. "I don't want a home. She wants me to stay in New York City all year long and care about the origin of bath towels."

Gavin doesn't have to say any more. I understand. We were both completely screwed up by our childhood, only in completely different ways. Gavin copes by running to the next adventure, never being serious, never staying long enough with anything or anyone to form a deep enough attachment to care if they disappear or disappoint. People like him because he's fun and exciting and always the life of the party. Lacey was the first person other than me to see Gavin for more than an irresponsible adrenaline junkie.

"Have you told her?" I ask.

He shakes his head. "She's in Uganda on a vaccine trip. Contact is spotty at best for the next few days. God. Look at her. She's a doctor, she's smart, she's sexy, she thinks I can run an international charity with her. It's insane. I...I moved too fast, I've only known her six months. I was an idiot to propose."

"Funny. I thought it was the smartest thing you've ever done."

He raises his eyebrow and I suddenly realize how annoying I look when I do the same thing.

"You say that because you want the Duporte merger." He wipes a hand down his face.

I shrug and shove my hands in my pockets. I'm in jeans and a long-sleeved T-shirt. I usually wear a suit when working, even at home, but not tonight.

Gavin leans his elbow on the counter and studies me. "You know, sometimes when I'm cliff diving or skydiving or doing some other inane thing, I envy you."

"Really?"

He nods. "You know exactly who you are, you know what you do. You're William Williams IV, CEO, business tycoon. Every day is laid out for you. Hell, the next 60 years are mapped out. You don't have to worry about a thing. No surprises. You have it made."

There's a hollow space in my chest that aches at his words. I have everything except the one thing I've always wanted most. I look away and roll the espresso cup between my fingers.

"I think, if you throw Lacey away, it'll be the stupidest thing you ever do." I say this with the certainty that comes from experience.

"Yeah. But I'm the stupid one, aren't I? Gavin's the stupid, fun one. Will's the smart, boring one," he says, echoing our father who always said it with a bitter laugh. Two halves, neither of them whole, he'd say. If only we'd been one boy, he'd have the perfect son, instead of two disappointments.

I set the cup down and it makes a sharp clinking noise against the counter.

"Anyway," Gavin says, "the envy only lasts until I land. Two seconds max. Then I remember you've worked eighty-hour weeks since you were 14 trying to please our bastard father. You saved his company, turned yourself into a machine, just so he'd say' good job,' but did he?"

I shrug. I stopped needing my father's approval years ago. I work now because I love it. Unfortunately, the consequences of striving to please him lasted longer than I could've imagined.

Gavin continues, "He approves of my wastrel life more than he approves of your business drive. Because at least I didn't show him up by saving his ass as a child. The hit to his pride was too much. He can't stand it that you did what he couldn't."

I smile ruefully. "Please wait until Lacey gets here for the engagement party before making a decision. Don't do anything you'll regret. She's good for you." I'd like to see at least one of us happy.

Gavin stretches then rubs his eyes.

"I'll think about it. But I'd rather have fun than think. Isn't this the town of love? Soul Mates, USA? I haven't been here in years, but I seem to remember there's a real hottie that used to stalk me with her eyes. Maybe I'm here to find my true love."

"No," I say. All the good, brotherly feelings vanish.

"What? She doesn't live here anymore?"

"Don't be an ass."

He narrows his eyes and looks me over from my too-long, needing-a-cut hair, to my jeans and bare feet.

"Dad did a number on you, Will. I remember when you used to be fun. When you laughed, told jokes and messed around. When you let yourself have friends. Jeez. Have you had a single friend besides me in the past twenty years?" He waves his hand dismissively. "No need to answer, I already know it's a no."

I clench my jaw and try not to think about Jessie sitting in the oak tree with binoculars hanging from her neck. I come back to work in Romeo dozens of times a year, a day or two every few weeks. Not because I talk to anyone or have friends here, Gavin's right, I have no one. I come here for her. Sometimes, just seeing her, Jessie, on the street, or in the store, makes me feel less alone.

And if she scowls at me, or says something cutting, I hold onto it like a treasure. Pathetic, I know. But I've known for 13 years that she only wants Gavin. She thinks she loves him and she has the opposite feelings for me.

Gavin says he's envious of me for two seconds at a time. I've been envious of him for a decade and a half.

If I had known when I was 12 how hard it would be to undo all the things I've done, I never would've started down this path. I didn't know that once you lose someone's friendship or respect, you often lose it forever. I didn't know once you start on a path it sometimes feels impossible to step off. Jessie has disliked me for so long, I don't know how the world would look if she didn't.

"I'm going to fix this," Gavin continues. "It's gone on long enough. Just because Dad said you were boring, barren of personality, and lacking a sense of humor—"

"Don't hold back."

"Doesn't mean he's right."

"Obviously." I raise an eyebrow.

Gavin grins. "Tomorrow morning, after I sleep off this

hellacious case of jet lag, we're heading into Love Town USA and breaking out the fun Will that's been hiding for twenty years."

"I'd rather not." I have an international business to run and a merger to complete.

"If you don't, I'll go have fun without you," he threatens. I think about the fun he'd find. Breaking my two-hundred-million-dollar deal in the process. He's got cold feet and Jessie has her arms wide open waiting for Gavin to run into them.

I've loved Jessie for as long as I've known her. The thought of her and Gavin together hurts worse than the thought of losing two hundred million dollars.

"What time in the morning?"

Gavin thinks for a minute. "Ten."

"Fine. We'll have some fun."

"That's the spirit."

I hold up a finger. "On the condition that you don't do anything stupid, don't mess with the process of the merger by talking to Alan Duporte, you don't break it off with Lacey while she's in Uganda, and you consider that maybe your own issues stem from Dad saying you were the stupid, fun-loving, irresponsible one."

"Yeah, yeah," Gavin says. He saunters out of the kitchen.

I make another espresso. I still have at least four hours of work to do tonight.

And I need to make a strategy on how to prevent Gavin from tripping and falling into Jessie's arms.

4

JESSIE

I'M ABOUT to take the first sip of my large triple shot iced mocha with extra whip cream and a cherry on top when I see him.

Gavin.

It's quarter to ten and I'm outside the SweetStop Bakery on Main Street. Romeo, in the soft morning light, with the sweet smell of cinnamon and sugar, is one of the most wonderful places in the world. But it's just taken on a sharper, more vibrant appeal.

My heart skips a beat. Not from caffeine—I haven't had any yet—but from the sight of Gavin in Romeo. It's been six years. He's thinner than Will, tanner, and he has a more restless energy, like he's waiting to spring into action. Which is perfect. I need him to spring into action when I trip and fall into his arms. I look down at my outfit, a vintage yellow and navy blue cotton pleated dress. It's about be sacrificed on the altar of love.

Gavin stands on the opposite side of Main Street, just outside the outfitters store. He's in hiking clothes and looks like a cover model for an outdoor magazine. He's reading something on this phone and pacing back and forth, oblivious to the morning activity of the town. Mrs. Charles pushes a cart of books out onto the sidewalk in front of Bookends, her used book store. Mr. Kwan stands on a ladder cleaning the hardware store's windows. Laney Forsyth has six dogs on leashes. She's beginning her daily round of dog-walking. She waves and I wave back.

Gavin still hasn't looked up from his phone, which is good. All I have to do is step in his path and let him run into me, spill coffee all over us, and let sweet love do the rest.

Gavin reaches the end of the storefront and turns around. He's focused on his phone, he taps something into it with his thumbs. He's only twenty feet away.

This is it.

Our meet-cute.

The moment our love story begins.

Well, I mean, for me it began when I was eight. But the story of *us* begins now.

My chest squeezes and I freeze—nerves. He so good-looking, so charming, so perfect. No. I can do this. As soon as we have our romantic-comedy-style clumsy girl meeting, Gavin will feel the soul mate vibes and fate will take care of the rest.

"You can do this, Jessie," I whisper.

Gavin's only ten feet away. His head is down and he's pacing toward me. I take a bolstering breath, hold my iced triple espresso, double whip mocha in front of me and stride forward.

Impact in three steps.

Two.

The glass door to the outfitter store flies open. I'm right in its path. I hold out my free hand to stop it, but it slams into me.

"Eeek!"

The door knocks me back and I spill the mocha down the front of my dress. The sticky ice-cold chocolate and whipped cream drink drenches the cotton. I gasp. The door hitting me *hurt*, and the coffee is *cold*. The door swings back and the man responsible steps onto the sidewalk. He looks at me with a stunned expression on his face.

"Jessie. Are you alright?"

My mouth falls open. "You...you..."

A glob of whipped cream slides down the front of my dress. Will watches its descent down my chest. I wipe it away and fling it from my hands.

"Are you okay?" he asks again. "Sorry. I didn't see you..." He trails off.

"I'm fine. It's fine."

I move past Will. Gavin is walking the other way again. He's talking on his phone now. I realize with surprise that he didn't even see me. Will opened the shop door in that one split second of opportunity and sabotaged our meet-cute.

"Can I get you napkins? Dry cleaning? Something to clean off with?" He starts digging in his pocket like he'll find a napkin in there. He's in outdoorsy clothes too. I haven't seen him in anything besides a suit in years. It's weird. And distracting. I scowl.

"Stop trying to be nice. It's confusing."

"What? I'm nice," says Will.

I widen my eyes in disbelief. He grins, flashing his teeth, and I remember all the articles that have called him ruthless.

"Fine. I'm not nice. I'm only offering to help so you don't bring a personal injury lawsuit against me or slander me in the news."

I tilt my head and my wet dress make a sucking noise. I grimace.

Will looks at my chest again and his eyelids lower, making him look sleepy and aroused at the same time.

In my fantasies, sometimes Will plays a role, always the

villain. Sometimes the fantasies get away from me and Will, the villain, captures me, ties me up, and does things...that I like. Those fantasies never make any sense. They confuse me.

Like now.

"Umm," I clear my throat and try not to notice my nipples tightening. It's the ice-cold mocha. Not Will's horny eyes. Clearly.

Gavin's a block away, talking on the phone, pacing near Mr. Kwan's ladder.

I have a moment of inspiration.

"Bye, Will."

I wave him off and hurry to the ladder. If I can climb up a few rungs and wait until Gavin passes, I can fall into his arms. It doesn't matter that I'm covered in coffee and whipped cream. I have a week to make love happen with Gavin, and I'm determined to give fate a helping hand. Plus, I don't know when I'll see him next without blatantly knocking on his front door.

It's now or never.

I grab the metal sides and step up onto the first rung. Gavin is ten feet away and heading toward me. I calculate that four rungs high should do it. I scramble up the ladder. When Gavin is only five feet away I let out a cute little planned squeak and wave my arms.

"Eek! Help!"

I lean back and peer at him from over my shoulder.

He doesn't notice. He doesn't even look at me. He's so involved in his phone conversation that he walks right by. Unbelievable.

What's a girl gotta do to get a guy's attention?

I twist around and take a step down. My stiletto catches on the rung. I grab at the ladder's edges, but I'm unbalanced. I shriek, it's not cute and it's not planned. I grab at the sides of the ladder, but my heel twists and I fall.

I hit—hard.

But it's not the pavement.

I hit a man's chest.

He wraps his arms around my back and my legs and pulls me against him. My stomach flips and I reflexively grab his shoulders. I take a breath. He's got me. Thank goodness.

Gavin saw me after all.

I look up into blue eyes.

"Thank you—" I start.

"What are you playing at?" he growls.

"Oh...you again..." I feel bad that I'm disappointed that Will caught me. Because he *did* save me. "Can you...do you mind putting me down?"

His eyes narrow and he gently sets me down. My legs wobble and I realize that the fall freaked me out more than I thought it would.

I look around and try to find Gavin. He's back in front of the outfitters store.

"You're up to something," says Will. He catches me looking at Gavin and his jaw clenches. Then his eyes narrow on my still wet, stained dress. Uh oh.

I flush.

"You were *trying* to spill your coffee."

My breath catches. "I was not!"

"And you were *trying* to fall."

"That's ridiculous."

"Is it?" he asks.

I feel my cheeks heat and they're definitely red because Will nods like I just failed his lie detector test.

"I thought we agreed. You're not Gavin's type."

I flush even more. The stickiness of the spilled drink on my skin is growing itchy and uncomfortable and I want to get out of this dress. My ankle has a pinchy throbby pain. I turn and limp away, trying to maintain a bit of dignity.

Not his type.

Bull crap.

Love doesn't have "types."

Gavin's finally off the phone. He leans back against the glass window of the shop and stares up at the clear blue sky. His shoulders slump and he looks tired and alone.

I know exactly how he feels.

I've felt alone since my mom died and my dad stopped speaking.

I keep myself busy from the minute I wake up to the second I fall into bed, so I don't have to think about the fact that I'm lonely.

Lonely and alone.

Gavin drops his head and I catch him quickly swipe at his face. Crying?

I want to reach out to him. Offer him my friendship.

More.

My back straightens and my determination comes back.

This is the moment.

I walk forward, my eyes on Gavin.

"Jessie." It's Will. He sounds sorry, like he's going to apologize. I ignore him.

"Jessie. Stop." He says stop like a command, not a request. "Stop."

I swing back around. "No. You stop."

I keep walking backwards, away from him. "Quit interfering —" I cut off when I hit a metal object.

Will reaches for me.

I grab at the object. It's books, stacks of books. Will grabs for me, catches my hand, but the book cart flips under me. I tumble over it and pull Will down with me. We crash to the sidewalk. I land on a pile of paperbacks. Will lands on top of me. The jarring thud sends a jolt through me and the shock of it stops all thought.

"Ow. Ouch."

Will groans. "That hurt."

"You're on top of me." I push at him, but he doesn't move. "Off."

He repositions himself so that his legs capture mine and his arms cage me in. He looks down at me and a calculating light enters his eyes.

"I'll get up when you promise to stop chasing Gavin."

I glare at him. "No."

He lets out a frustrated breath. "I'm not going to let you ruin his chance at happiness."

The nerve.

"What if I'm that chance?"

"Not possible," he says.

I glare at him and then push up against him, trying to dislodge his bulk. His blue eyes go dark like the deep, violent blue of the Romeo River before a storm. The depth in them scares me, like I might drown in the stormy waters, never get air and never come up again if I dive beneath the surface. He lets out a short huff of air and the black of his pupils dilates. Suddenly, I have the urge to reach up and brush the lines at the corners of his eyes, touch his long feathery eyelashes and see if they feel as soft as they look.

He makes a low sound in his throat. I look at his mouth and focus on his plump lower lip, soft and wicked...so at odds with Will's personality.

Will.

William.

I gasp and wrench myself out of my lust-filled stupor for the wrong man.

"Get off." I shove at him again. He blinks and shakes his head, like he's trying to reenter the present.

Yeah, welcome back from Weirdville. That alternate dimension where Will and I lust after each other.

Ugh.

Why?

I have a week with Gavin in town, I don't need Will confusing things.

"Look, Jessie." He shifts, but doesn't let me up.

I squirm under him and peer toward the outfitters store. Gavin isn't even there anymore. Unbelievable.

"No. You look." I shove my hand into his chest. I ignore the fact that it's a surprisingly well-muscled chest. "Gavin and I are meant to be. Miss Erma predicted it."

His body stiffens and he shakes his head, once, hard in denial. Of course he'd disagree.

"She's. Never. Wrong," I say.

His jaw clenches and his eyes narrow. "I. Don't. Care."

I push up on my elbows and lean into him. My chest presses against his and I bring my lips close to his ear, so he can hear every word.

"I'm going to do everything in my power to show Gavin we're meant to be."

I let the words hang between us. My lips are so close to him I could nibble his ear without moving an inch. I feel it the moment his heart picks up speed—it thumps against my chest.

He turns his head and his jaw brushes against my mouth. I pull back and he smiles. I stay on my elbows. He leans forward until our lips nearly touch. His hips press into mine and this moment is so similar to one of my nighttime fantasies that certain parts of me clench in anticipation.

"Promise?" he asks. I feel the heat of his breath against my lips.

I want so badly to span those few millimeters and press my lips to his. And that's what makes me realize—he's taunting me. Teasing me. Laughing at me. That's what Will does. What he's always done.

I remember when I was twelve, when he and Gavin finally came back to Romeo after four years gone. I saw Will outside this very bookstore. I thought maybe he'd changed. I asked him if he'd ever heard of Narnia and handed him a copy of *The Horse and His Boy*. I'd just bought it. I'd read it a dozen times at the library and I'd saved and saved for my very own copy. Will looked at me and then at the book.

"You can have it," I said with a small smile. A friend was worth the weeks saving up for a book. I could save money again, but a friend was priceless.

Then his dad came around the corner. He was in a three-piece suit and shiny black shoes.

"Who is that?" he asked Will.

I blushed and looked down at my ratty, too small, secondhand tennis shoes.

"I don't know. A nobody," said Will in a strange crisp voice that made my chest hurt.

His dad frowned at me, so I looked down again. His suit had the brightest gold buttons. I wondered if they were real.

"Come on then. We have dinner with Congressman Gillihan and I wanted to hear about your latest theory on..."

They started to walk away, but then Will hesitated. He must've realized he still held my book in his hand.

"What's that?" his dad asked.

Will paused, and I strained forward to hear his answer. He looked toward me, a quick dismissive flicker of his eyes, then he shrugged.

"Garbage."

Then he tossed my book in the public trash can.

My chest felt like it was cracking open. Will and his dad strode away, not looking back. I ran to the trash. The flap on the door kept me from being able to reach deep enough. I couldn't get my book back. I held back my tears and choked down the lump in my throat. It was just a book. Only a book.

I knew I used the characters as substitute friends, as a way to make my silent house seem full when my dad went weeks without saying one word.

But still, it was only a book.

I could get another. It didn't mean anything that Will had thrown me...my book away.

I walked to the library and surrounded myself with the words and dreams and company of a thousand stories.

I blink and look up at Will. The edges of the used paperbacks dig into my back and legs. My chest feels achy and cracked open again. I don't know how he does it, but Will always manages to find my broken spots, pry them open, and let out all the ghosts.

Enough.

I'm done with him interfering in my life.

"Not only do I *promise* to show Gavin we're meant to be. I guarantee it." I raise my chin and give him a challenging stare.

He blinks and his demeanor changes. He becomes less languid wickedness, and more the hard, ruthless, cold-hearted CEO that I know and don't love.

"Then I promise," he says in a low hard voice, "to do everything in my power to stop you." His upper lip curls. "I guarantee it."

Of course he does.

Of course.

That's fine, Will doesn't have the power of fate and a library of hundreds of romcoms behind him.

Love wins. Every time.

This is Romeo after all.

It's on.

5

WILL

GAVIN and I spent the day white-water rafting. He spoke to Lacey on the phone outside of the outfitters store. He didn't say what they discussed, but since he seemed to have a death wish on the raft, I'll take a wild guess and say it wasn't anything good. He chased each roaring bit of river and foaming white rapids he could find with single-minded desperation.

"Now that was fun," Gavin says. He clinks the neck of his beer bottle against mine.

I take a long swallow of the ice-cold beer.

Gavin continues, "See what I mean? You need to have fun. Live a little. I think there was one point I actually heard you laugh."

I take another swig of beer. That time he's talking about, I wasn't laughing, I was choking on the frothing rapids that splashed over the edge of the raft.

"Life can be fun if you go out, grab it, and wrestle it. Look around you. Fun!" Gavin gestures around us.

We're standing in an open green space, a rectangular park near downtown Romeo with a short grassy lawn, flower beds in full bloom, and mature shade trees. This park is where they hold their festivals and celebrations and town events.

Like the event tonight.

The Summer Sweetheart's Dance.

There's local New York cider, wine and beer. Food stalls selling hot dogs, burgers, grilled corn, and pulled pork for various local charities. And a dessert table manned by The Friends of the Library.

"Fun," I say.

I try to get a closer look at the dessert table. Did I see Jessie or was that someone else in a yellow dress with black hair?

I'm usually uncomfortable at this type of event. I don't know what to do, where to stand, who to talk to. It would surprise everyone except Gavin, but I'm not good at talking to people, especially people I don't know. That's why I love finance and business. I can talk numbers and ROI and profits and losses with anyone. When I was nine, my father realized I could compute a thirty line balance sheet in my head in seconds. I remember, before that day, I played outside, made friends, I missed my mom, but I got by. After that day, my father became obsessed with finding out what I could do, and how much I could learn.

At first, I fought against the daily afterschool tutors that drilled me from four until nine and the hours of economic theory and business reading lists. I'd often sneak out to ride my bike. So my father took off the wheels and left the frame in the front yard as a reminder of what happened when I disobeyed. I'd hide books to read for fun, under the covers at night with a flashlight. He'd find them and the books would disappear. I'd spend mornings throwing a ball for my dog, Riley, a Jack Russell my mom gave me before she left. One day, I came home and Riley was gone. There was a new morning economics tutor in his place.

The friends I once had disappeared too. If he saw that I invested in someone more than learning, he cut off the friendship. Often cruelly. He even did his best to pit Gavin and I against each other.

If ever I showed I cared about something or someone more than business and economics, they were somehow destroyed. So, I did the only thing I could to protect them, I didn't let myself care. And if for some reason I did care, I never let them or him know.

"Is father coming to the engagement party?" I ask.

"Nah. The bastard's in Dubai with his latest mistress."

"That's good," I say. He retired when I turned eighteen and forced him to cash out his ownership in the company— Williams and Williams, our family's international accounting firm.

He passed ownership on fifty-fifty to Gavin and me. It was his last attempt to pit us against each other. It didn't work.

If Gavin ever wants to step in and take a roll, he can, if not, that's fine too. I disburse profits at the end of the fiscal year and both Gavin and I share in what our great-grandfather started. One thing my dad never understood about me—I care more about the people I love than about business or a hundred million dollars. Or maybe he did understand, which is why he worked so hard to remove everyone I cared about from my life. He wanted a business prodigy and then he hated it when he got one.

I look over at Gavin. I truly believe he and Lacey are meant for each other. He loves her, I can tell. He could also use her stability and support. She seems to see him for who he truly is. A good person. But...

"Look, Gavin. If things don't work out with Lacey, I'll figure out the business side." It'll be hell, but I'll figure it out. I care more about my brother than a merger.

Gavin sighs, nods, then looks away. "Those were some rapids, huh? Almost as sweet as this time in Queensland on the North Johnstone River. I took a helicopter out through this rain forest with volcanic gorges to class V rapids. It took six days to raft and at night it was like I was in another world. The mushrooms at the base of the trees glowed in the dark and there were luminescent insects floating in the canopy." He smiles at me. "We should go there."

Even though the trip today was not my kind of fun, the look on his face makes me agree. "Deal. After the honeymoon."

Gavin turns to the open lawn. A bluegrass band warms up on a small wooden stage and couples move toward the grassy dance area marked out by hanging lights. It looks like the Summer Sweetheart's Dance is about to begin.

"Alright," says Gavin. A fast song begins and the mandolin player's fingers fly. "Dang. Who is that?"

I turn and look toward the woman he's nodding at. And I realize it couldn't have been Jessie at the desert table. Because tonight she's in a lipstick-red dress and her hair is a long loose black cloud of temptation. She sways under the hanging lights and her eyes are bright and luminous.

When she sees Gavin looking her way, she smiles and it's like I'm trying to look into the sun—she's so beautiful that it hurts.

After I learned my dad would take away or destroy anything I cared about, it was easy to hide my emotions and pretend I didn't have any. That I didn't care about anyone at all. In reality, it didn't take too many years until that became my truth. I shoved every emotion down until I didn't feel anymore. I stopped caring.

Except with Jessie. It always hurt to see her and pretend I didn't care, or worse, didn't want her. When we were fifteen and Jessie made it clear she wanted Gavin and was disgusted by me,

I should've been happy for them both. Happy my father would definitely never see how much I wanted her. But it made an angry abyss roar inside me. Right now, it's roaring again.

I see the way Jessie looks at Gavin.

He straightens and rolls his shoulders.

He sees it too.

Like hell they're meant to be.

Like hell this Miss Erma person is never wrong.

I may never have been able to tell Jessie how I feel and I may have screwed up my chance with her years ago, but that doesn't mean I'll stand by and watch her chase my brother.

I turn to Gavin. "Hold my beer."

6

JESSIE

I KNEW I had fate on my side. Why else would Gavin be at the Sweetheart's Dance? While I was getting ready, choosing between the green dress or the red, I sent up a prayer. I said, *if this is meant to be, please let him come to the dance.* And here he is.

So.

It's meant to be.

Gavin's across the green grass of the open field. He's in a tight T-shirt and he looks rugged and lean. His hair sticks up a bit like he's been out on some windy adventure. Will stands next to him. My skin tingles and I chalk it up to irritation. Of course he'd be here too. Unlike Gavin, he's in a button-down shirt, his hair is smooth, and he looks as starched and uptight as ever. The thought of yanking his buttoned shirt open flashes through my mind. I shove it away.

The band starts to play, the fiddle player holds a long note, and then the mandolin comes in—the notes fly fast. I take a step towards Gavin.

He's in an animated conversation with Will. Gavin gestures

excitedly with a beer in his hand and Will gives him a wry smile.

I take another step and stop at the edge of the lawn under the string of white lights. In nearly every romcom movie, there's a moment when the man sees his woman in a new way. Their eyes meet, music swells, and there's a reaction. I call it the long stare.

"Look at me," I whisper. "Come on. Long stare for the win."

The long stare is the second-most common way couples recognize their connection. An awesome meet-cute was number one, but that didn't quite work out.

The bluegrass music picks up and segues into the perfect song for couples to dance to. I start to sway. Then, thank you fate, Gavin looks up. He sees me. His eyes widen. He says something to Will.

Will looks at me, and something flickers in his eyes, but it's replaced by a black look. His warning fills my mind. But it doesn't matter, because Gavin looks at me again. From across the lawn our eyes meet. The lights twinkle, the music swells and—*yes*—Gavin and I are doing the long stare.

Any second now he'll feel the connection. In fact, any second now I'll feel something, that lightning strike of awareness.

Just one more second of—

Will shoves his beer in Gavin's hand and steps in front of him.

A flare of annoyance fills me. I step to the right and try to see past Will. He steps with me. I clench my jaw and step to the right again. Will moves with me. I step twice to the left. Will moves with me. He completely blocks my view of Gavin. His lips turn up, and his eyes glitter, he shakes his head at me. Telling me no.

"No," he mouths.

"Yes," I say.

He's twenty feet away, steadily moving toward me. I step left, he mirrors me. I move right, he moves too. All the while he holds my gaze. His eyes lock on mine and I can't look away. I keep moving and he moves with me. We're in some sort of strange dance that's taking place a field apart. Every time I try to look away, break away, there he is again, pulling my eyes back to him.

Until all there is, is the music, the lights and me and Will.

I shake my head no.

He nods his head yes.

Suddenly, he's in front of me. He stops less than a foot away. Entirely too close. I lift my chin so I can keep holding his stare. I won't be the first to back down. With Will, you can't show any weakness; he'll take advantage of it. Every time.

"What do you want?" I ask, holding his gaze.

His eyes widen and the blue of his irises darkens. "What do I want? I thought I made that clear." His voice is low and intimate with a note that makes me feel like he's running his fingers over me. I flush and his lids lower over his eyes until he has the look that I associate with my forbidden fantasies. I have the overwhelming urge to tell him yes, I agree to everything he wants. Everything. Anything. His dark eyelashes flutter and I think I see equal longing in his eyes.

I take a shallow breath and try to regain my equilibrium. Then, I realize that Will and I have been holding our gaze for easily more than a minute. And what he made clear, what he wants, is for me to let go of my soul mate.

The warm, deliciously wicked feeling breaks.

"Ack. No." I break eye contact, shake my head and look away, out over the lawn and the dancing couples.

"That bad?" asks Will sardonically. He puts his hands in his pockets and looks at a group of kids running in circles around their dancing parents.

"You ruined my long stare." I'm feeling put out and off-guard.

"Is that what that was?"

"Of course. The long stare is like the clumsy girl meet-cute, or walking down the stairs in a flowy dress, or a first kiss in the rain. It's—"

"A bad cliché?" He gives me a boyish half-grin, like we're sharing a joke.

I sigh. It's funny, even though Will has been my nemesis for twenty years, it's times like this that make it hard to hate him.

"Why weren't we ever friends?" I ask without thinking.

Will's relaxed boyish demeanor vanishes and is replaced by the cold, stiff façade that I'm used to. Here's the Will that's capable of shutting down any attempt at friendship.

When we were fifteen years old, Will found me in the branches of the oak tree. It was dark, eleven o'clock at night, and I thought he was Gavin. I sink into the memory.

It's a moonless night and the sky is like a dark blanket with a hundred stars poking through the blackness. The crickets are singing and I'm reading by flashlight when he climbs up. I'm not scared. I'd heard him coming from the big house from across the field. When he climbs up I scoot over and give him room on the wide limb. My heart beats erratically. Gavin is here —he's finally come back to our tree. He turns his face down towards my book, but he doesn't say anything.

"It's *The Voyage of the Dawn Treader*." I hold up my book. I've read it so many times that I can recite entire paragraphs from memory.

He smiles and moves next to me until our thighs touch. My legs are cool from being out in the night air for so long. He's so hot I can feel the heat of him to my core. My stomach flips and my mouth goes dry. I don't know what to say, he's finally here again, after seven years. He rarely comes to Romeo, and when he does it's for such a short time. I thought he'd forgotten me.

"I saw your flashlight," he says.

I startle at the sound of his deep voice—so different from the last time I heard him.

"Sorry. Did it bother you?" I click off the flashlight and wait for my eyes to adjust to the dark.

"No." He shakes his head.

I peer at him through the darkness. He's tall, his arms and legs are long, and his shoulders are wider than they were the last time I saw him. My cheeks heat and awareness of his leg pressing against mine floods me.

He doesn't say anything more, so we sit in silence and listen to the night sounds. Finally I feel the tension I hadn't realized was there seep out of him. He relaxes into the curve of the tree limb and leans toward me until our arms touch. The feel of him runs over me and I shiver.

"Cold?"

I shake my head. "Not really."

But he still slowly reaches over and puts his arm around my shoulders and pulls me close. My heart thunders in my chest and my breath comes out in short pants. I can barely stand the feelings coursing through me. I think I might burst.

We're sitting in our tree, there are brilliant stars and the grassy perfume of the field, and Gavin's arm is around me. This is better than my dreams.

"Are we still friends?" I whisper, driven by seven years of dreams dreamed in a silent house.

He stiffens slightly, a warning, but I don't really register it until much later. I'm too caught up in the closeness of him.

"Last time you were here...the day my mom died..."

He turns and looks at me, his face is inches from mine, and

even in the dark I can see the deep blue of his eyes. He looks tired, there are bags under his eyes, and a heavy weight in his gaze that a fifteen-year-old shouldn't have. But I understand it.

"My dad hasn't said more than fifty words in seven years. I don't have friends here. I..." I hold up my book. He doesn't look at it, he keeps watching me.

"I read so I don't remember how lonely I am," I say. I'm taken by surprise when a tear slips down my cheek. "I'm lonely."

He watches me and suddenly I'm uncomfortable with my confession, with opening up so much to someone I only met once before. When I was eight. For heaven's sake, I've had three dozen awful run-ins with Will, but only one beautiful moment with Gavin. And this moment.

"Say something," I whisper. His eyes are shadowed and tired and filled with deep regret and self-recrimination that I don't understand.

"I'm sorry," he says.

There's so much sorrow in his voice that I can't help it, I lean forward and I press my lips to his. He stiffens in surprise, but instead of pulling back like I thought he would, he stays where he is. His mouth is warm and his lower lip is soft and full. I'm finally having my first kiss. With Gavin. In our tree. It's more perfect than I could've ever imagined.

I reach up and touch his jaw. My fingers stroke over his skin. His lips soften even more and I try to move closer. I let out a small sound against his lips. When I do, he pulls back. I blink up at him, wrapped in the heat of him and the drunken excitement of my first kiss.

"That was..." I shake my head, try to clear it, and smile at him. "Gavin...that was..."

I can't explain it, it was more than words. I finally felt connected again. I knew he'd come back. I knew he felt it too.

"I'm not lonely anymore," I say, and so much gratitude and happiness wells up inside me, I feel like I could fly into the night sky and shine with the stars. That's how happy I feel.

"Gavin, do you think...will you come here tomorrow night? We could..."

He pushes away from me and slowly draws the back of his hand over his lips. "Jessie," he says, and the mocking tone of his voice sends a prickling of alarm down my spine.

I squint and try to get a better look at him. His upper lip curls into that sneer I've seen a hundred times. I gasp and my blood goes cold.

When he sees the look on my face he lets out a low, horrible laugh.

Oh no. No no no. I cover my face with my hands. I told him my secrets... I felt connected to... I had my first kiss with...

"Will," I choke out.

He wipes his hand on his pants and sneers at me. "To answer your first question, no, we aren't friends."

I gasp and panic bubbles inside me and burns at the back of my throat.

It's Will. It's Will. It's Will. The words thud over and over in my mind. He looks down and gives a small smile at my tightly clenched fists.

"We'll never be friends," he says.

I look away and quickly swipe my eyes. "Stop it," I cry out. "You're horrible. Why would you trick me like that? Why would you do that?"

Even in the dark, I see his face go white. "Because that's what I do. Because I wanted to," he says in that horrible, clipped, unemotional way of his. If he'd spoken in more than monosyllables earlier, I'd have known it was him right away. If it hadn't been so dark. If...

"You're a creep. You're an awful, horrible creep, you always have been and you always will be."

He shrugs, uncaring. "To answer your second question, no, I won't be coming back for more. I run an international company, I don't play with children, and I don't need friends. Unlike some."

My nails dig into my palm. The jerk. The jerkity jerk.

"From the day I met you, I knew you were awful."

"Really? When we were eight?" He sounds surprised. It seems like I've managed to shock him out of his contempt.

"Yes. Even then you liked to hit me when I was down. You were rotten."

He gives me a contemptuous look.

I glare back. "Fine. Yes, *William*, I kissed you tonight. But only because I thought you were Gavin. He's fun and kind and...and everything you're not—"

"So they say," he says dryly.

"So, get out of my tree." I fling my hand out and gesture for him to leave.

He tilts his head but doesn't move. "And if I told you that my mom died last week, and I just needed somewhere to go to be quiet?"

I look over at him and feel regret at my words. "Did she really?"

But he must hear the note of skepticism that I can't keep out of my voice because he lets out a small laugh.

"No. See you later, Jessie."

He drops from the branch and out of the tree. I don't watch him walk away, but I can hear him move through the tall grass, back to the dark, old, cavernous house.

I found out later that month that his mom really had died the week before Will came up the tree. But both he and Gavin were already gone by the time I heard. They didn't come back for almost a year.

"We were friends when we were eight," says Will, bringing me back to the Sweetheart's Dance and the here and now.

I shake my head. "What? No."

He shrugs. "Agree to disagree."

"We'll disagree." Then, "You stole my long stare." Gavin is across the clearing, buying desserts from the Friends of the Library fundraising table.

"If you think staring at my brother like a cow with a stomach ache is going to catch him, then you're deluded."

I cough. "I'm a cow now?"

He holds up his hands as if to say...yes?

"You also stole my meet-cute." I hold up a finger. "The coffee." I hold up another finger. "The ladder." I hold up a third finger. "And falling over the books."

He grins.

I remember him sitting in the tree with me—kissing me.

"And..." I poke him in the chest. "You stole my first kiss."

He looks at me in surprise, then chokes back a laugh. "When we were fifteen? You kissed me! I didn't steal anything. You practically attacked me."

A heated flush washes over me. He has a point, but...

"I thought you were Gavin. My soul mate."

The laughter fades from his eyes and his mouth turns down. He takes a step toward me and there's a look in his eyes that I don't like.

I glance over my shoulder back toward Gavin. He's eating a pile of Miss Erma's oatmeal raisin cookies, chatting with Juliet at the wine table. Will clears his throat. I look back, surprised to find him so close.

His bottom lip curls into a wicked smile and I realize why his look made me nervous. It's predatory.

"What are you doing?" I ask.

"Stealing your first dance."

Then he takes me in his arms and spins me into the circle of dancing couples. He spins me away from him and then back to him again. Gavin's watching us. So are the ladies at the dessert table. Gavin smiles. Will pulls me closer.

"Eyes on me," he says.

"I'd rather not."

Will laughs and then bends me backwards in a fast dip. I gasp and he pulls me back up. He pulls me close, our lips almost touch, but he spins me in another circle and leads us through the dancing couples.

My friend Chloe and her husband Nick are dancing. Chloe sees Will and me together and her eyes widen. Veronica is nearby, and when she sees us dancing, she does a double-take then steers her husband the other way.

In fact, it looks like the whole town is watching us dance. Our mutual antipathy has never been a secret.

"Everyone's watching," he says, mirroring my thoughts.

"It's like they smell blood," I say.

He gives me a toothy grin and twirls me again.

It's true. Our dance is more a battle than not. I pull away, he spins me back. I push, he catches. I fall back, he pulls me up. He spins us until the lights and the people are blur and all I can do is focus on him.

"Smile," he says. "You're supposed to smile when you dance."

"Screw off," I say and I bare my teeth at him.

He chuckles deeply and it sends vibrations down low into my abdomen.

The music picks up speed and he puts his hands around my waist, picks me up and spins me around. My dress flares out around me. I gasp at the warmth of his hands spanning my ribs and the ease with which he lifts me. He slows and pulls me close. When he sets me down my front drags along his. My breasts press against his chest.

He holds me close, his hands span across my lower back and rest in the hollow that feels like it was made for him. He looks down at me and my heart thunders in my ears. It takes me a moment before I realize the music has stopped. I step out of Will's arms and he lets me go. His hands fall to his sides and his expression shifts back to closed-off and cold. I shiver and turn back to Juliet's wine table.

"He's gone," says Will, the teasing is gone from his voice.

"What?"

"Gavin left while we were dancing."

I turn and quickly look around the field, but I don't see him. Not anywhere.

"You did that on purpose."

He nods. "I told you, I'll do whatever it takes. Even dance."

I shake my head. "I don't understand you."

He shrugs. "You don't have to."

"You know, you won't always be there to stop me. Fate is going to intervene, Will. You can't stop something that's meant to be."

"Because the psychic love lady told you it was fate?" he asks with annoyed disbelief.

"Exactly."

"So we're still doing this?" He gives me a challenging stare.

"If you mean, am I still following my chance for true love and are you still trying to stop me, then yes, we're still doing this."

"So what's on for tomorrow then? An impromptu song in the park? A contrived emergency so Gavin can play hero?" He raises a supercilious eyebrow.

I shake my head. "Good night, Will."

He smirks. "See you tomorrow."

I hold back a smile. "Looking forward to it."

And strangely, I realize that I am.

I have big plans, and I don't think even William Williams IV will be able to stop me.

7

WILL

I DECIDE it's time to be more proactive. I'm looking for Jessie, I have something to give her. I step into the air-conditioned, book-scented hush of the Romeo Public Library. Even though I've known for years that Jessie works here, I've never been inside. It seemed like too much of an intrusion of her privacy. Or, let's be honest, I didn't want to see her smiling and happy in a place she loves and then have that smile replaced by wariness and dislike.

So, I avoided the library. It was better to see her at the wine bar, or the bakery, or walking on the sidewalk. If she noticed me then, and I managed to react to her as I always have and act like a cold-blooded ass, then it didn't feel so bad, her shift to adamant dislike.

I walk into the library and look around. It's about the size of two school classrooms. The ceilings are high and vaulted with wooden beams. There are large arched windows looking over the Romeo River, rocking chairs, magazine stands, and a puzzle table where a man and a boy sort through small puzzle pieces. To my right is the circulation desk, where you can check out books. There's an older white-haired woman behind it, but not Jessie. I wander farther into the library. There are long rows with shelves and shelves of books. The children's section has a dress-up area, a play kitchen, a train table and a huge cushioned chair. A mom and her two boys are in the chair reading a picture book. The younger boy looks up and waves at me. I hold up my hand and wave back.

I wander through the shelves and run my hand over the cool spines of the books. I breathe in the deep smell of old paperbacks and taped book bindings. There are about a dozen people here, but it's as hushed as a winter's morning after a heavy snow.

I've circled the library but I don't see Jessie. I wonder where she is. It's three o'clock and I know she works until five on weekdays. I look down and rub the worn cover of the thin paperback in my hand. It's my favorite book, I've read it so many times that I've had to glue and tape and re-glue the binding. The cover is torn into three different places and I think in a few years the book may fall apart beyond repair.

I sigh and head toward the circulation desk, book in hand.

"Excuse me."

The white-haired woman behind the circulation desk looks up from her reading and smiles. She pulls off her pink and purple reading glasses.

"Checking out?" She looks at the book in my hand.

"No. No, this isn't a library book. I'm looking for Jessie."

The woman smiles and her eyes crinkle. "You must be Gavin."

What the...?

I shake my head. "No. I'm his brother."

I lean forward and try to look friendly when I'm feeling anything but. "Is she expecting him?"

She clicks her tongue against her teeth. "Well, we all are,

aren't we? After Miss Erma announced him as Jessie's soul mate. Congratulations on your brother's match." She smiles.

I show her my teeth and hope it looks like a grin and not me grinding my teeth together.

"Miss Erma predicted my soul mate. My Eddie and I have been together for thirty-five years next month. She's never been wrong, dontcha know?"

I clench my teeth harder and my jaw tightens. My paperback bends in my hand and I quickly loosen my grip on it.

"I'm sure she's been wrong at least once or twice."

The woman clicks her tongue again. "Oh no. Never. She's never been wrong. She's successfully predicted hundreds of matches."

I nod. What a crock, who would believe this garbage? Except...Jessie, and from what I hear, the entire town. Including Jessie's friend Veronica and her husband Sam.

On his mission to bring back the "fun me," Gavin and I went rock climbing this morning. We ran into Veronica and her husband Sam, and decided to climb together. Well, everyone else climbed, I mostly fell, since I've never been climbing before. The entire time, Sam kept giving Gavin and I speculative looks, and Veronica flat out took me aside and told me if I messed up Jessie's chances at love, she would tie me up and drop me in a cave so dark and deep no one would ever find my body. Her husband Sam overheard the threat. Instead of being concerned, he laughed, kissed her and asked if she'd tie him up and throw him in a cave.

Insane.

Then Sam took me aside and asked about hiring a few project management consultants out of my New York City office. The whole time Veronica gave me the side-eye and as I left she gave me the "I'm watching you" gesture.

Don't mess things up for Jessie and Gavin, she'd said. Which meant, this white-haired librarian, Jessie, Veronica, Sam, and apparently hundreds of couples believe in this soul mate psychic baloney.

The hollow space in my chest aches again. Maybe she isn't wrong. But I said it once and I'll say it again. I. Don't. Care.

When I was eight, I fell for Jessie. Maybe the psychic says there's someone else for her, but there's no one else for me. I found Jessie before I stopped being able to care and I never was able to let her go.

I decided after rock climbing that I need to finally step off the path I've been walking. I'm going to be who I've always wanted to be around Jessie. Gavin's right, I've been what my dad made me into for too long.

"Will Jessie be back before you close?" I ask the librarian.

She clicks her tongue. "She's already here. She's teaching the seniors' computer skills class in the community room." She points to a pair of wooden double doors near the children's area.

"Thank you."

I step into the community room and quietly closed the double doors behind me. Jessie is bent over a computer next to an eighty-plus-year-old man in a flannel suit.

"You push the control and C keys at the same time to copy, Mr. Frank," she says. "Or you can find the copy command in the edit menu."

"Aha. I was pushing control and Z."

"That puts the computer to sleep," says a steel-haired woman in a purple muumuu.

"Nonsense, Petunia. Control Z reverses your last action," says a tightlipped woman in a gray collared shirt.

"It was a joke, Gladiola, even after seventy-seven years you still can't understand a joke."

"I'd like to control Z your conversation," says Mr. Frank.

"Who is this?" says a woman with short tight white curls and large horn-rimmed glasses.

All four seniors and Jessie turn and look at me.

"I'm William. Mind if I join?" I smile at Jessie and ignore the glare that she sends my way. "Looks like you're having fun."

Petunia looks at me and my nonchalant smile and then at Jessie's stony expression. A mischievous light enters her eyes. I get the impression Petunia likes a good joke.

"You can share my computer," Petunia says in a chipper voice that would scare a veteran soldier.

"Thank you." I start to walk across the room to the long computer table.

Jessie scowls and marches toward me. I take a moment to admire the way her cheeks go pink and her black hair swings almost angrily and her blue-gray dress swishes around her legs like the tail of an annoyed cat. There's fire in her eyes and I smile at the spark.

"What are you doing here?" she hisses. Then her eyes widen and she looks behind her to make sure no one heard. All four of the seniors are staring openly at her, completely fascinated.

I wink at Petunia and she snorts.

"Stop it," says Jessie to me. Then she leads me to the other side of the room, farther away from our audience.

"What do you want?"

I swallow. The book is heavy in my hand. Somehow this is even harder than I imagined. But every journey has to begin with a first step.

"I came to give you a book."

"Okay. Fine." She shrugs and holds out her hand.

There's a tight thudding in my chest. Opening our Hong Kong office last year wasn't this stressful.

I gently place the book in her hand. My back is to the room and I'm shielding her from everyone's eyes. Her fingers close around the book and she stares down at the torn, worn, faded cover.

"What...?"

She doesn't recognize it. For some reason I thought she would. I know it looks different than the last time she held it. It's much worse for wear.

"I wanted to give it back." My voice is quiet. "You said it was your favorite. It's my favorite too." I hold my breath and wait for her response.

She turns the book over and gently opens the cover. BookEnds, Romeo NY, is stamped on the first page. She runs her finger over the stamp, and I watch her, transfixed.

"But...you...you threw it away. I saw you."

"I went back for it."

I don't mention how I stayed up until two in the morning waiting for my dad to go to bed. How I sprinted the miles to downtown praying Jessie hadn't dug it out, and praying the garbage collectors hadn't come. I don't tell her how when I pulled it out of the trash I started to cry. I hadn't cried in the four years since my mom left. I didn't know why I cried then. I stayed up the rest of the night and read it, then read it again.

This book let me imagine Jessie and I were friends. As long as I had it, I could keep on pretending.

"Why?" She searches my face.

Here goes. "I thought about what you said. I think we should be friends."

She looks down at the book and shakes her head.

The hollow spot grows bigger at her no.

"Sorry about the state of it. I read it a lot. I underlined a few places too. Passages I liked. Sorry."

She looks up and a small laugh escapes from her lips. She

stifles it. Then, "What? Cretin. I should've known you were the type to write in books."

She takes the book and holds it against her heart in an unconscious gesture. I smile as relief washes through me.

"Friends?"

She strokes the worn cover of the book and I think of all the times I held it.

"Does this mean you won't stand in my way?"

I shake my head. "No. It means that I'd like to be friends." There's no way I'll help her pursue my twin brother. That's a special hell I'll never willingly enter.

She wrinkles her brow and studies me like I'm a mixed-up jigsaw puzzle.

"Okay," she finally says and I feel my shoulders relax. I let out a relieved breath.

"Friends," she says, and she smiles at me. I'm blinded by the radiance of it.

She walks back toward her seniors computer class and I follow, watching her skirt swish around her hips. She turns back.

"You can't stay for class. Seniors only."

"Oh darn," says Petunia. "I was going to pinch his bottom when he sat down."

Gladiola scowls. "Hush, Petunia. He can't be here. We're helping Jessie get ready for her big date."

Jessie groans, and I swing around and look at her. She looks away from me nonchalantly. It's so obvious, she may as well be twiddling her thumbs and whistling.

I casually turn back to Gladiola. "Big date, huh? Jessie and I are friends. Surprised she didn't tell me."

Gladiola deepens her scowl. "Pshaw. I wasn't born yesterday."

But Mr. Frank decides to help a fellow man out. "Jessie has a date with her soul mate. They're going to Tybalt's for dinner. I bet he'll seal the deal. That Tybalt's is the hotspot for romance." He wiggles his eyebrows meaningfully at me.

I swing around and narrow my eyes on Jessie. She purses her lips and raises her eyebrows.

Petunia speaks up. "They're having the spaghetti. Jessie called Chef Renaldo and he promised to keep the noodles extra-long so they can reenact that scene from *Lady and the Tramp*. You know, the kissing scene."

I give Jessie a hard stare. When, amidst our rock climbing day, did Gavin manage to agree to a date?

I turn to Petunia. "What time is dinner?"

"Oh, seven," she says happily.

I give Petunia a big smile, then turn to Jessie. "Have fun tonight."

"What are you planning?" Her eyes narrow on me.

"Nothing. Nothing at all."

I hurry out. I have a lot of planning to do.

8

JESSIE

"TELL US ABOUT GAVIN," says Gladiola. Senior computer class is over, and the three ladies—Mr. Frank went home to watch a sport fishing competition—are helping me with my plan for tonight.

"I don't want hear about Gavin. I want to hear about William," says Petunia. "Hotdog! Those stony, buttoned-up businessman type are freaks in the bedroom."

"Petunia! Her soul mate is Gavin. The brother," Gladiola snaps.

Petunia and Gladiola are sisters, seventy-eight and seventy-seven years old. They live with their ninety-six-year-old mother, Iris. Petunia and Gladiola were both widowed in the last five years.

"Well, is Gavin just like his brother? Because, woo dee, the amount of repressed sexual energy buttoned up under that business suit is off the charts. The sex appeal was rolling off him. I bet that William is the type that needs it at least twice a day. Minimum." Petunia fans herself.

"That's vulgar," says Gladiola.

"Please, don't tell me your suit-wearing, stiff-lipped Rodney didn't come home revved up after a day in court, ready to pound the gavel."

For a second Gladiola smiles, then her eyes cloud over, and her hands shake as she pulls a tissue from her sleeve. She rolls it into a ball and stares at the floor.

"I'm sorry, Gladiola." Petunia reaches toward her sister. Gladiola waves her away.

"Tell us about Gavin," says Wanda. She lives at Water's Edge Retirement Center and brought Miss Erma with her last class. She takes off her horn-rimmed glasses and wipes them on her bright polyester flower print blouse. Wanda is a peacemaker, it probably comes from having four daughters and eleven grandchildren. One of her granddaughters is Juliet—the owner of the wine bar.

I look at Gladiola and make sure she's okay. She puts the tissue back in her sleeve and smiles at me.

"Well..." I dig the toe of my high heel into the short-pile moss-green-colored carpet. I sigh. What can I tell them about Gavin to help them understand why he's right for me?

"Is he also a tiger in a suit, waiting to rip off his buttons and eat you?"

"Umm..." I feel my cheeks flush red. I think of Will and the way he sometimes watches me.

"Not at all. They're complete opposites."

"Hmm. Sad," says Petunia.

"Stop that. William isn't her soul mate, Gavin is. Stop making trouble," scolds Gladiola.

Petunia sticks her tongue out at her sister.

"Lord help me," says Gladiola.

"Go on, dear," Wanda says.

"Well..." I drag my toe over the carpet. "Gavin is always smiling and laughing. He makes people comfortable, even those who are usually shy in public. He can make any situation fun. His smile—"

I think about the years I counted every single smile he ever gave where I could see him. Seven smiles when he was twelve. Twenty smiles at age thirteen. Eighteen smiles when he was fourteen. And zero smiles when he was fifteen. That was the year his mom died, although I didn't know until after he left Romeo.

"His smile makes me smile." I look up from the carpet at their expressions.

"That's wonderful, dear. What's he like when you talk?" Wanda gives me an encouraging nod.

My neck prickles. I can count the number of times we've spoken on one hand. I know how ridiculous it seems to have wanted him for so long without ever really speaking to him. But...

"Well, we haven't talked much." I press my hand my stomach. "But...the day my mom died..."

"I remember," Wanda says.

Gladiola nods. "We were there. You ran off. Your father was desperately worried."

I look up in surprise. I never knew he even realized I was gone. "I ran home. When I got there, Will was there, he shoved me into a mud puddle."

Gladiola lets out an angry humph. I lift a shoulder. I don't know why Will does what he does. Not when he was eight, not now.

"Gavin found me in the puddle. We climbed a tree together, and he told me since both our moms had left, we could be friends. I was crying so he gave me his handkerchief."

"Oooh, dashing," Petunia says.

"What kind of eight-year-old carries a hanky?" Gladiola asks.

"Shh," Wanda says.

I go on. "I gave him a flower and we sat together. And suddenly the worst day of my life...there was a light in all that dark. And all the years after, when it got dark again, I only had to think of that time or take out that handkerchief, and I knew that everything would be okay. Even if it didn't feel like it at that moment."

He was my beacon in the darkness.

"Ahh. A childhood marriage promise. I love it," Petunia says.

I roll my eyes and smile at her.

Gladiola's forehead is furrowed. "You haven't spoken since you were eight?"

"Not really. I sort of idolized him from afar." I flush and realize how idiotic that sounds. "Stupid."

Wanda shakes her head. "Not at all. You had a fantasy. Why risk disappointment from the real thing?"

Was that what I had done? Not approached Gavin because I didn't want to break the image I had of him?

"But now Erma said he's Jessie's soul mate, so he'll be better than she imagined," Petunia says. "You can throw out your perfect fantasy and discover the real man. Trust me, real men are more interesting and more fun than perfect fantasies."

Wanda nods. "That's a fact."

"Enough talk. Let's get down to business," Gladiola says.

She pulls an old brown leather suitcase out from under the computer table. Petunia rubs her hands together in excitement.

"Are you sure about this?" I ask.

Gladiola yanks the suitcase's zipper open and pulls out a hand-beaded black dress with a V-neck that looks like it'll go down to my belly button. I swallow so loudly I think everyone can hear my gulp.

"Like you said, makeovers are the bread-and-butter of

romance." Gladiola pulls out a pair of five-inch gold high heels. She's not done. Out comes a lacy garter belt, silk stockings, a strapless push-up bra, and...

No way.

"I've changed my mind. The real lesson in romcoms is that it's what's on the inside that counts. You know, I'm beautiful on the inside, and I love myself...no waxing, hair straightening, glasses replaced with contacts, or sex kitten outfit necessary." Not that I have curly hair or wear glasses, but still. "Since Gavin is my soul mate, he'll love me for who I am, not what I look like."

Petunia lets out a cackle, and I realize I've let loose three evil fairy godmothers. When I asked them to help with my date tonight, I didn't think they'd go this far. I like my classy 1950s career woman outfits.

"Here's some wisdom from someone who was married for fifty-two years," Petunia says.

"Oookay." I don't know if I'm ready for this.

"Men are visual creatures. Give your man a small teaser trailer of the upcoming blockbuster. Let him obsess over the trailer, imagine the blockbuster. You aren't giving him the main event, you're giving a teaser."

"I don't know, Petunia." I hold up the dress. "This looks like the entire show."

She shushes me. "I wore that dress to the opera in 1960 and got a marriage proposal that night."

"The advertising executive? You didn't marry him!" Gladiola says.

"All the same," Petunia says. "You'll be just like Cleopatra in this dress. Irresistible."

I grimace. "Please don't say that. Cleopatra married her brother. Then when he died, she married her other brother, then she 'cheated' on her brother with Caesar, most likely killed her brother, then hooked up with Mark Antony and then offed herself. She's *not* a good example." I look at the dress and its shimmery beads. "I'm not wearing this."

"But Cleopatra ruled the world," Petunia says.

"Uh huh."

But I give in. They can do my hair and makeup and pick out my outfit. Gladiola owned a salon, and Petunia owned a boutique. Even at nearly eighty years old they know style. And since I only have a few more days left with Gavin before he leaves Romeo and possibly gets married, I need to make an impression.

I frown. I hear Will's voice. *"He's getting married. Leave him alone. I won't let you ruin his chance at happiness."*

Am I ruining his chance at happiness? Gavin picked his fiancée. He didn't pick me. Fate did, I think. But he didn't. Is free will, the choice of who you'll marry, necessary for happiness? Would he rather his choice of a partner, even if she isn't his soul mate, over me? Because he chose her. An arrow of guilt lodges in my chest. I sit still as Gladiola curls my hair into a French twist.

"What makes a happy marriage?" I ask.

Gladiola tugs on my hair and my eyes water.

Petunia hums as she brushes blush onto my cheeks. "Sex. A wise woman doesn't let more than a few days pass without sex."

Gladiola scowls at her sister.

"Fine. I'll be serious." She picks up the mascara and I can tell she's about to impart fifty years' worth of wisdom.

"Tell your man you love him, that you're proud of him and grateful for all he does. Support him, treat him with love and he'll do the same for you. Tell him what you want and need—be specific—don't make him guess. Men aren't good at guessing."

"That's a fact," Wanda says.

Petunia pulls out a tube of lipstick and continues.

"Be loyal to him, give him understanding and love. Be the kind of partner to him that you want him to be to you." She pauses and looks at the other women. "It goes by fast. There'll be hard times, fights, illness, lost jobs, lost houses, deaths. Such hard times. But beautiful times too. Ask yourself, not, do I want to spend my life with this man when things are great, but, is this the man I want to be with when everything is going to hell and we're both falling apart? When love is a memory, and the sex is nonexistent, because that will happen, for a spell—"

"That's a fact," Wanda deadpans, and they all laugh.

Then Petunia continues. "When love is a memory, will you remember that family and loyalty and support and kindness and compassion and friendship are something you hold dear? Can you sit together, stay, hold hands through hell and let the love blossom again? Because that will happen too. Ebbs and flows. Remember, if you don't value yourself, and know who and what you love and stand for, then you'll fall for anything and lose everything. Think about it. Love isn't only about the good times and happy feelings. It's about the hard, dull, day-to-day times too. It's fifty years of good mornings, not just one night of candlelight."

I let Petunia's words sink in. Fifty years is a long time and it won't all be filled with candlelight and flowers and first kisses. That's fine. It's not what I've dreamed of. What I fantasize about is waking up and the space in bed next to me is warm, not cold. Or being at the grocery store and picking out a box of cereal that I know my husband likes. Or coming home after a long day and instead of hearing only silence, hearing him in the kitchen or watching TV, and knowing that I'm not alone. Knowing someone out there cares...about me...and I care about them.

Petunia pats my shoulder and steps back from me. "You're ready."

Wanda holds up a hand mirror. "What do you think?"

My eyelashes look longer, my lips fuller, my hair is shiny and sleek. The smoky eyeshadow makes me look mysterious and womanly.

"I don't recognize myself."

"You look like your mother," Wanda says.

My heart thuds and I give her a grateful smile. "Thank you."

"I never told you, I'm sorry we didn't see how much her death affected your father. We didn't see how bad it was until you were grown. We're very sorry," Wanda says.

"We all are," Petunia says.

I nod and squeeze Wanda's hand. "It's okay."

My dad died three years ago, but it didn't hurt nearly as much as it should have. Because it was as if he'd been gone years before.

"Well, it's time we're off. Enough chitchat. We have to set up the rain shower," Gladiola says.

"Nine o'clock sharp outside the bakery?" asks Petunia.

"That's right. We'll be there," I say.

The ladies are helping me with an impromptu shower for a movie-worthy kiss in the rain. I wonder if William will try to stop it. I smile at the thought. I bet he's suspicious about this evening. I'll never admit it to Will, but I tricked Gavin into meeting me. I claimed I wanted to interview him about his travels for the next library newsletter. When I mentioned dinner at Tybalt's, he happily agreed—apparently spaghetti and meatballs with garlic bread is his favorite meal.

I let out a deep sigh. "I'm ready."

Tonight, Gavin and I will have dinner, he'll finally see me as his one true love, and we'll have a romantic kiss in the rain.

It will be perfect.

9

WILL

At twenty minutes after seven I stroll into Tybalt's Italian restaurant. I wanted to be early, but I had an emergency phone call from the head of the Shanghai office. I hire people I trust to put out fires on their own, so when I get an urgent call, I know I'm needed. It took nearly two hours to remedy the tangle and put the right people in place. I hung up at ten minutes after seven. Then it took me all of ten minutes to shower, throw on a suit, and speed to downtown Romeo. I had to park a few blocks down, it's busy tonight. At first I walked fast, then I figured, the hell with it, and I sprinted down the sidewalk to Tybalt's. I slowed to a walk when I neared the restaurant, smoothed back my hair, and adjusted my tie. When I pushed open the heavy wood front door I was only slightly out of breath.

I look around the dimly lit dining room. Tybalt's is fine Italian dining. It's been in the same family for four generations. When I was a kid, it served big family-style spreads, huge plates of freshly made pasta and just-out-of-the-oven focaccia sprinkled with parmesan and rosemary. The latest owner went and studied culinary arts in Rome, then Paris, and came back to make Tybalt's a Michelin-starred family-style Italian restaurant. Like Mr. Frank said, it's where you go in Romeo when you want romance to happen—engagements, anniversaries, first dates.

"Welcome to Tybalt's. Do you have a reservation?" The hostess smiles and reaches for a stack of leather-bound menus.

The dining room is crowded, nearly every table is full. I scan the room, it's dimly lit by crystal chandeliers and candlelight. The light reflects off the silverware and white tablecloths. There's a quiet hum of happy conversation and clinking silverware. The familiar smell of warm yeasty bread, rosemary, garlic, roasted meats and seasoned vegetables fills the air. The last time I was in Tybalt's, seven years ago, Jessie sat near the back. I look past the diners toward the table for two nestled in an alcove in the back corner.

"I see my party," I tell the hostess.

I stride through the dining room. Neither Jessie nor Gavin notice me. They lean toward each other, Gavin speaks animatedly and Jessie listens with a happy, open expression on her face that she's never given me. I pause. They look like a couple. Jessie leans closer to Gavin and her arm brushes against his shirtsleeves. Gavin gives her a wolfish grin. The candlelight shines on the black of her hair, coloring it the blue of a hot flame. She blushes and looks down at the table. There's a bottle of wine, a plate of bread, and a large plate of spaghetti placed between them.

A plate to share.

The scene of those two darn dogs, slurping up the spaghetti and kissing, hits me. This is a seduction scene, no doubt about it.

I catch the look on Gavin's face and alarm bells go off in my mind. I know that look. He gets it right before he's about to do something horribly self-destructive.

Whenever things are going well in his life and it looks like he might succeed, be happy, or come out on top, he gets this look and does something to sabotage it all. This look is the precursor to every school expulsion, failed business venture, and ruined relationship in his life.

Dang it all.

Jessie glances up at him and the light flashes on the beading of her dress. Gavin's eyes dip to the low vee showing off her... I swallow... her breasts.

Dang it all to hell.

I unclench my fists and walk forward, grabbing an empty chair on the way.

"Gavin. Jessie. Funny running into you too. Mind if I join?"

Gavin tears his eyes from Jessie's chest. He looks at me and his brow wrinkles in confusion.

"Uh, hey Will...um, no?"

"Yes," Jessie says at the same time. "Yes, we do."

"Great. Thanks," I say. I situate my chair across from Jessie and drop into it. The table is meant for two, it's a tight fit.

Jessie's red lips purse together. I remember in old cartoons they'd make steam blow out of characters' ears with a train whistle sound when they were really mad. I never understood that graphic until now. Jessie literally looks like there could be steam coming out of her ears.

I grin at her.

She lets out a low growl.

I turn to Gavin. "I didn't know you guys were friends. You should've invited me along. Jessie and I go way back."

Gavin's eyebrows lower, and I can tell he's trying to work out what's going on. I see it the second he decides that I'm here to keep him from making a mistake he'll regret. Like he said, I don't have friends.

"I thought you were in the throes of fixing some crisis in

Shanghai." He turns to Jessie and smiles his suave grin. "My brother here has been known to miss two, three meals in a row. He forgets to eat when he's in the middle of work. Remember that week in Tokyo? I went out to the...uh...to have some... uh..." He gives a side-look at Jessie and realizes what he did in Tokyo isn't fit for polite company. "I, uh, when I got back Will was nearly passed out on his desk. The idiot hadn't eaten or slept in nearly 48 hours. That Tokyo deal was hell for Will."

I grab a piece of warm focaccia and dip it in the olive oil, avoiding the searching look Jessie's sending my way.

"Right, Will?" asks Gavin.

"Mhmm." I shove the bread in my mouth and let the flavor of rosemary and parmesan spread over my tongue. Really good.

"That was when we were 17. Will was still trying to dig Williams and Williams out from under its mountain of debt, get his degree, and prove to our father that he was—"

"Have some focaccia," I say to Jessie. I hold the plate out to her. "It's delicious."

"No thanks." She gives me a tight smile. "You were saying," she asks Gavin.

I shake my head at Gavin, but as usual, he ignores subtle hints. Instead he focuses on the encouraging smile that Jessie gives him. He doesn't want her, not really. I know my brother and I can tell he loves Lacey. He isn't interested in Jessie. Thank God. Unfortunately, that fact isn't as clear to Jessie. She's still trying her darnedest to make Gavin see her as his true love. I scowl. Not happening.

"Right. What was I saying? I guess just that Will's lucky he has me. Because otherwise he wouldn't eat, or have conversations that don't involve business acronyms, or get out and have fun."

"He's definitely lucky to have you then." Jessie gives Gavin a sugary sweet smile. I catch her eyes and raise an eyebrow.

Gavin turns his attention to the wine, pouring himself another glass.

Jessie takes advantage of his inattention.

"Leave," she hisses at me.

"You look beautiful," I whisper back.

Her cheeks flush pink. "Go away," she whispers.

"What did you say?" Gavin asks.

"Oh. I just wondered how you like the spaghetti?" Jessie flutters her eyelashes at Gavin and I try not to scowl.

Gavin picks up his fork. "It's delicious. It reminds me of the pasta I had at a little family restaurant in Capri."

"Oh wow. I've never been. Sounds amazing." Jessie picks up her fork and drags it through the long noodles. She waits until Gavin starts to roll spaghetti around his fork then she moves her fork trying to capture his moving noodles.

I'll be...

She might actually pull off this noodle kiss farce.

I watch the noodles on her fork go taught. She smiles in triumph. Gavin doesn't know it, but their noodles are connected.

He starts to raise his fork to his mouth. Jessie raises hers in anticipation.

No way.

I grab my fork and quick as I can I slash it through their joined noodles. Jessie gasps. I take the noodles and shove them in my mouth.

Gavin laughs. "You really are hungry."

I chew loudly. "Mhmm," I say through my mouthful, "starved."

Gavin goes for another bite and Jessie drags her fork through the plate and tries to capture the ends of his spaghetti.

"You were telling me about your adventures. I'd love to hear more," she says.

Gavin lifts his fork to his mouth. I grin as a single noodle of his slips through Jessie's fork.

"Jessie's going to do a travel book article in her next library newsletter. She wants to use my experiences as a basis for it," Gavin says to me.

I perk up. "This is a work dinner?" That's interesting. Jessie hasn't been honest with Gavin.

"Funny, right?" Gavin says. "I've never had a work dinner and even when you try not to, here you are, at another one."

"Hilarious," I agree.

Jessie won't look me in the eyes.

The waiter comes by with another wine glass and the menu. I assure him I'm content sharing the family plate of spaghetti.

Gavin launches into a story of ballooning in South Africa. Jessie nods and smiles and tries her hardest to pretend I'm not here. I keep my eyes on her. It's not hard. I could watch her for hours and never grow tired of it. Gavin is entering the exciting part of the story, the bit about the lion and the jeep, when Jessie finally breaks. She subtly turns my way.

She points at me, and then makes the "get out of here" gesture with her thumb.

"And then the lion jumped over the..." Gavin continues.

I raise my eyebrows and point to myself, feigning confusion.

Jessie nods and makes the "get out of here" gesture again.

I shake my head, look around, and pretend I don't understand.

"And that's how a jeep and a baobab tree foiled a lion and saved my life," Gavin says triumphantly.

Jessie looks at him in confusion, while Gavin looks at her expectantly.

"Oh. Ah. Wow. That's amazing. I never heard anything like that. The baobab. Wow." She flushes bright red.

I hold back a smile. She wasn't listening, not at all. I'd bet my bank account on it. She was too focused on me.

"Tell the story about Cambodia," I say.

Gavin nods. "That's a good one."

He moves to take another bite of spaghetti, then stops with his fork hanging in the air. "It was six months ago. I was hang gliding over the jungle, there were some ruins I wanted to see."

Jessie watches his fork move up and down. He finally goes to twist his fork in the noodles. Jessie follows.

"...the snakebite burned. I had minutes..." Gavin is wrapped up in the memory of meeting Lacey. He doesn't notice that once again his and Jessie's forks are attached by a ridiculously long noodle.

But I notice.

So does Jessie.

I reach forward with my fork, ready to cut the noodle.

But Gavin moves his fork up off the plate. Jessie's eyes widen. She sees my fork coming, so she shoves the spaghetti in her mouth. She starts to suck in the long noodle. I watch it pull taught. Gavin is oblivious. His fork is six inches from his mouth.

Jessie's eyes are wide. Her lips purse as she pulls on the connecting noodle.

The freaking noodle trick is going to work.

I don't stop to think. I drop my fork and grab Gavin's and I shove it in my mouth.

"Hey! What the heck, Will?" Gavin says.

I suck on the noodles. They pull taught and one long sauce covered noodle dangles between Jessie and me.

Triumph fills me.

The noodle between our mouths gets shorter as I suck, pulling us closer. I suck harder. Tug.

Jessie moves forward, closer to me.

Then she panics. She jumps up from her seat. Swipes at the

noodle and breaks it in half. Her movement flips the plate of spaghetti over and the noodles and sauce fly onto her dress.

Oh no.

The clattering of the dish on the floor sounds loud in the hushed restaurant. Everything stops as people turn to look at our table.

Jessie stands stunned as noodles slide down the front of her dress.

"And that is how my life was saved and I met my wife-to-be," says Gavin into the silence.

Jessie turns to look at him, shocked.

He grins and shrugs.

I come around the table. I pull the pocket square from my suit pocket and dip it in the glass of water.

"Here. Let me help."

The waitstaff rushes over, ready to help clean up.

Jessie looks down at her sauce-covered chest and then back up at me. I hold out the handkerchief like a truce flag.

"Here use this."

There's a glint in her eyes. She ignores the handkerchief. "You...you..."

She grabs a handful of noodles resting between her cleavage, and I watch as she hefts the handful and smashes it into my chest.

I look down at it in surprise. Her eyes light with satisfied glee.

Behind her, I hear Gavin begin to laugh.

"I won't dignify that with a response," I say.

She smirks, grabs of glob of sauce from her collar bone, and smashes it against my cheek.

Gavin's laugh is full belly now. "Having fun, Will?"

I ignore him. "That wasn't nice."

Jessie grins at me, and I'm so distracted by it that I don't see her reach around and smack a handful of spaghetti against the back of my head. It runs down my collar under my shirt. I jerk back in shock. Jessie watches my expression, then it seems she can't hold it back anymore, because she begins to laugh. I feel a smile form as I watch her wipe tears of laughter from her eyes.

"Here." I hold up the handkerchief and gently wipe away the streaks of tomato sauce and happy tear tracks from her face. I carefully draw the fabric over her skin. She stands quiet and still, her eyes watchful.

Gavin clears his throat. "I'll help get this cleaned up. You two should head out and get changed."

It seems that Jessie suddenly remembers where we are and that she's trying to impress Gavin. Her face flushes as red as the tomato sauce.

"No. I mean, I'll stay—"

I cut her off. "You're right, Gavin. Thanks."

I grab Jessie's purse and her arm and pull her to the front door.

"But...but..." she protests. When we make it to the sidewalk she spins out of my arm and shakes her finger at me. "You're unbelievable."

I raise my hands. "Me? Why? I'm just doing what I told you I'd do."

She stares at me, mouth open, dumbstruck. Not for long though.

"This isn't what friends do," she says.

I raise an eyebrow. "I disagree. Friends save each other from making stupid decisions."

She turns away and starts marching down the street away from the restaurant. I follow her. Her spine straightens when she hears me.

"He's not interested in you. Couldn't you tell?"

"No." She turns toward me and a noodle slides off her and lands on the sidewalk. "I couldn't tell because you interrupted. He may have been interested, he may have felt that spark, but you sabotaged it."

I throw my hands up. "For crying out loud. He was telling you the story of how he met his fiancée. That is the epitome of a man who is *not interested*."

She slows down and I think maybe I'm getting to her. But then she lifts her chin and walks faster. We cross the street and near the bakery. It's closed this time of night, it's almost nine o'clock.

"I'm going back to the library, getting in my car, and driving home. Tomorrow, I'm going to get up and try again. No matter what you say and no matter what you do."

"Jessie. Don't be a fool." It's only been two days of this madness, well two days and two decades, but I want so badly for it to stop.

"A fool? Who is the fool? I finally found my soul mate. I'd be a fool not to go after him. Okay, maybe he doesn't want me, or like me, maybe he doesn't see me, but he *could*. If I don't try, then what? *Then* I'd be the fool." She slows her pace and comes to a stop at the bakery window.

"Sometimes I wonder, if even my soul mate doesn't want me, then who will?" Her voice breaks and I see her sitting in the tree, telling me that her mom's gone, that her dad doesn't want her, and that she's all alone. A tear trails down her cheek and she angrily wipes it away. She turns her face away from me. I feel unequal to this moment. I don't have the words. Me, I want to say, you'd have me.

"I..." I begin. She looks at me and I swallow the lump in my throat.

"I know. You don't have to say it. I'm a fool. He's getting

married, he's not interested, I'm not his type, blah, blah, blah. I know." Her voice breaks again, and I want to reach out to her.

"But you know what?" she asks.

I shake my head. "What?"

"I disagree. I believe in love. I believe in fate. And even if I have to get drenched in coffee, or spaghetti, or...whatever...I'm going to keep trying. Because..." She pauses, then tilts her chin up and continues. "Because I have a lot of love to give. A lot. And I've been waiting my whole life to give it to that boy I fell in love with a long time ago. So...so there."

I don't say anything. I just stand there and take in the passion coloring her cheeks and the spark in her eyes. I want her so badly it hurts.

A water drop hits me in the forehead. Then another. Jessie looks around, and an expression of shock then guilt comes over her. The sparse drops turn to a light shower. Jessie closes her eyes and groans.

"Jessie?"

She shakes her head. I look around. It's raining in a five-foot circumference around us. I look up. Petunia and Gladiola wave gleefully at me from a second-story window. Wanda holds a large sprinkler over us. A suspicion enters my mind.

"Is this a kiss in the rain?"

"No," Jessie says. She opens her eyes and peeks at me. "Turn it off," she shouts up at the ladies.

I take a step toward her. "Were you going to lure my brother here for a romantic kiss in the rain?"

"No. Of course not." She takes a step back. "Turn it off, Wanda," she shouts up.

"Can't hear you, dear, I lost my hearing aid after class," yells Wanda.

"She said turn it up," Petunia says.

A slow grin spreads over my face. I take another step

forward. Jessie takes a careful step back. Water runs down my face. I wipe it from my eyes. Strands of hair are starting to fall out of Jessie's French twist. I reach forward and brush a lock off her cheek. Jessie takes another step back and bumps into the brick bakery wall.

The rate of the fake rain shower increases. Water pours down around us. Drops stream over Jessie's face and onto her dress, washing away the spaghetti and sauce. I put my forearms to the brick wall on either side of her, closing her in. I bend down, until our mouths nearly touch.

"Did you think a kiss in the rain would make him fall in love?"

"No." Her eyes turn dark and luminous. A drop of water trails down her cheek and settles on her lip. I groan. I've never ached to taste a drop of water so much.

"You want to know who would want you, Jessie?"

"Who?" she asks reluctantly.

"Me."

I press her against the wall and send my lips to hers. She gasps and her mouth opens to me. I send my tongue in, I run it over her lips and drink the falling water and the taste of her.

I press my body over hers and shield her from the rain. I bury my hands in her hair and pull her closer. She makes a small sound in her throat and I lick it up. I take her lip in my mouth and tug, then I send my tongue across her lower lip. She's heaven.

She was right. If I didn't already love her, then this kiss in the rain would make me love her for forever and beyond.

Her hands settle hesitantly on my shoulders and I groan. I need more. I need more of her. It's been too many years since I've touched her. It's been too many years of wanting her and not having her.

I grab her hips and pick her up. Her dress rides up and she

wraps her legs around me. I press her against the brick wall. She's positioned in the perfect spot. I rub against her and she gasps. I jerk my hips and she gasps again. I catch the noise with my mouth. I run my fingers down her cheeks, rock my hips against her and catch another cry in my mouth.

"Jessie," I say against her lips. I kiss the corner of her mouth. "I want you. I'll always want you."

She stops moving. Her hands tighten on my shoulders.

I pause. "What is—"

The sprinkle of rain water turns into an ice-cold flood as three 10-gallon buckets of water pour on my head.

I sputter and cough. The shock of cold runs through my system. I manage not to drop Jessie.

"Save it for the wedding night, Lothario!" shouts Petunia.

Freezing cold replaces the drunken warmth of Jessie's kiss. I clench my jaw to keep my teeth from chattering. I look down at Jessie. Her expression is...enraged?

My chest tightens and worry stampedes through me. "Are you okay?"

"Put. Me. Down." She shoves at my chest.

I lower her to her feet and steady her on her high heels. She's soaking wet. The beaded dress clings to her, outlining every curve. Her hair is loose and wet around her face. She shivers and wraps her arms around herself.

The window to the second floor slams shut. Our audience is gone.

"Don't ever do that again," she says, voice cold. She shivers again.

I swallow. It hurts to take a breath. I pull off my suit jacket, the outside is wet, but the inside lining is still dry.

"Here," I say. I put it around her shoulders.

She shakes it off and hands it back. She starts walking.

"I'll walk you to your car," I say.

She scowls and I think she's about to say no, but then she concedes.

"Alright." She starts toward the library, her heels click on the sidewalk.

"I meant what I said," I say in a quiet voice.

She shakes her head. "I know you said you'd do anything to keep me from Gavin, but this is low, even for you."

It takes a moment for her words to sink in. She thinks... "You think I'm trying to seduce you to keep you from Gavin?" Disgust fills my voice.

She sighs. "I don't know, Will. What else would it be?"

We've made it to the library parking lot. The tall streetlamps flood the lot with light. Jessie's hatchback is the only car in the lot. The quiet of the night settles around us. We stand in the lot and watch each other.

Water drips down her face. I pull the damp pocket square from my pocket and hold it out to her.

"Here."

She takes it and wipes her face then starts to hand it back.

"Keep it," I say. Then, "You know, I'd control Z the past if I could." I'm quoting her computer class—control Z erases your past actions.

She gives me an odd look.

"I wouldn't. Then I wouldn't be me."

"That'd be a shame," I agree.

She lets out a short huff of breath. "Night, Will."

The lamplight spills around us and I don't want to leave her.

"See you tomorrow," I say.

She rolls her eyes. "Do we have to?"

I nod. "Obviously."

"Maybe you should talk to some people around town.

86

They'll convince you that Erma's soul mates are real. Then you can leave me alone."

I raise an eyebrow. "Why would I want to do that?"

She snorts. Then she climbs in her car, shuts the door, and drives away.

I watch her tail lights until they disappear.

10

JESSIE

"LET ME GET THIS STRAIGHT," says Veronica.

We're all at the bakery for a morning coffee and emergency girl chat called by moi. Chloe, Veronica and Ferran sit around an outdoor table on the sidewalk. The white and blue striped table umbrella shades us from the morning sun. Tall ceramic pots full of red and purple and pink flowers surround the outdoor seating area. It's seven in the morning and downtown Romeo is just starting to wake up.

"Okay," I say to Veronica. I take a bite of my apple fritter. The coating of white sugar glaze cracks as I bite into it and melts on my tongue. I know donuts are terrible for your health, but this morning I don't care.

Veronica gives the side-eye to my Romeo Public Library book bag stuffed with romance novels. "For the past few days you've been going gung ho after Gavin."

"Ye-es," I say, stretching out the word.

"And Will, the man you love to hate—"

Alarmed indignation washes over me. "I do not—"

"Has been gung ho after you." Veronica wiggles her eyebrows at me.

I drop the apple fritter to my plate. "What are you saying?"

"She's right," Chloe says. "You do love to hate Will. You have for years. Every time you see him or his name is mentioned, you get all hot and bothered."

"What? That's not hot and bothered... it's..." I wave my hands in the air. "It's dislike. Mutual dislike."

Ferran puts down her mega jug of coffee. She's a coffee fanatic. "I'm pretty sure him making out with you against that wall"—she points to the brick wall ten feet away—"means the dislike is *not* mutual."

We all stare at the wall for a moment. I feel my cheeks flush. While my mind is saying *no way*, my body is saying *wheeeee*, like it's on some deranged lust roller coaster. The way Will backed me against the wall and held me in place while he moaned into my mouth is apparently just what my body has been waiting for.

My body wants more.

I shake my head. "He promised to keep me from Gavin, it's just a game to him."

Chloe looks skeptical. "Are you sure my aunt said Gavin was your soul mate? Because she can be kind of opaque in her predictions."

My stomach flutters, then does a cartwheel. "No. She did. It was clear. She said my soul mate was the Williams boy I'd loved since I was a kid."

"Gavin," says Ferran.

I nod. "Gavin."

Chloe bites her lip in thought. "Hmmm. I just thought, maybe..."

Across the street, Chloe's husband Nick runs by, pushing their baby Ava in a running stroller. Ava's in a frilly dress and a sun hat and she waves her arms and giggles. Nick grins at Chloe as he runs past and Chloe snaps a picture with her phone. We all take a second to soak up the cuteness of Dad and baby out for a morning run. After they've disappeared past the bridge we turn back to the conversation.

"So, you've tried a dance, a long stare, a makeover, romantic dinner, a kiss in the rain...what's left?" asks Ferran.

"Desperation," I say.

I grab the apple fritter and shove another bite into my mouth.

"His fiancée." I swallow down the growing guilt, "Gavin's fiancée gets here on Saturday for their engagement party. So I need him to realize I'm his soul mate before then."

Chloe frowns. "I don't like it. Take it from the woman left at the altar by her cheating fiancé, it's not...it's a really horrible thing to do to someone."

Veronica reaches over and pats Chloe's arm.

"It worked out though," I say. "Because your fiancé wasn't your soul mate. In fact, you should thank your second cousin for marrying him so you could find Nick."

"A soul mate pronouncement doesn't give you the right to hurt other people," says Chloe. "Be careful that you don't do something you won't be able to forgive yourself for."

I look down at the crumbs of my apple fritter. The sugary pastry sits heavy in my stomach. I haven't met Lacey yet. It's been easy to forget her existence, or push her aside as "not right for him." But what if I'm wrong? What if she's as kind as Chloe, or as loyal as Veronica, or as determined and smart as Ferran? This woman I've never met, she doesn't deserve her heart broken.

"I..." I look at my friends. "I texted Gavin this morning and asked if he wanted to go mountain biking."

There's a long moment of awkward silence, then, "You need to borrow a bike?" Veronica asks.

"Yes, please," I say quietly.

Veronica has three mountain bikes, two Specialized, and a Trek. She took up mountain biking after college for when she needs something more exhilarating than rock climbing.

"He's only here for a few more days," I say. "I've never followed my feelings for him before. I was always too scared or too shy or too whatever. I know the timing sucks and it looks..."—I glance at Chloe—"really bad. But I just want to put myself in his path and let fate do its thing. If it doesn't, and Gavin keeps looking at me like I'm his kid sister—"

"He did?" asks Ferran.

I shrug. "Pretty much."

"That's weird," says Veronica.

I shrug again. "If nothing clicks for him, then I don't...I have to try."

Chloe sighs. "What a pickle." Then she looks at Veronica. "Vee, I just got the best idea for a pickle card."

Veronica perks up. "Nice. Pickles, huh? I could sell that."

"I have to go," says Chloe.

We wave her off. Once inspiration hits, she doesn't have room to think of anything else. She jumps up and hurries to her office. It's in the loft above the bakery, where the senior ladies sprinklered Will and me from last night.

"I've got to get to work too," says Ferran. She gulps the last of her coffee. "If you ask me, you should figure out if you actually love Gavin or if you just really, really want to."

There's a tightening in my chest at her words.

After she's gone, Veronica turns to me. "So...bike?"

"Yeah," I say. "Thanks. Let's do this."

She smiles. "It handles light, and since it's your first time, be careful. I don't want you to break any bones."

"Do you think I'm doing the right thing?" I ask.

Veronica studies me, then shrugs. "I ran from my soul mate, and fate caught up with me. You're chasing yours. I'm sure it'll all work out."

She sounds sort of doubtful.

MY TEETH CLATTER AS I STEER THE BIKE OVER A MAKESHIFT LOG bridge. My helmet strap digs into my neck and my head knocks about as I ride over a pile of rocks strategically placed on the path.

"Whooo," shouts Gavin. "This is awesome!"

I wipe at the sweat dripping into my eyes and attempt to keep my bike upright. My favorite kind of exercise is walking. It may have been a tad ambitious to invite Gavin mountain biking. Gavin hits a ramp and his bike soars for a second before landing on the dirt single track.

"Don't you love it?" he shouts.

"Love it," I squeak. I brake to a stop and awkwardly scoot my bike over the ramp. Behind me, Will snorts.

"Think that's funny?" I ask over my shoulder. "Let's see you do it."

Will is ten feet back. He's riding one of Gavin's old bikes. He has on a helmet, bike gloves, and a pair of shorts and a T-shirt that shows off his bulky shoulders and biceps.

When I arrived at the mountain bike trail, Gavin was already there with Will and two bikes. I wasn't surprised to see Will. Of course my traitorous body started to cheer.

Gavin said that Will had been working since three in the morning, and since it was eleven, he'd already put in a full day. Which meant Gavin felt obligated to drag Will from the office and make him have some fun. Gavin said "fun" with a weird emphasis. I smiled and agreed that Will did need to loosen up and have some fun. Will looked at me with a wolfish gleam in his eyes. A gleam that made heat rush to my cheeks.

The Romeo mountain bike trails are on the ski slopes outside of town. The ski lodge converts the slopes to bike trails during the non-snow sport months. For the first half-mile, Gavin stayed close, telling stories about other bike trails he's been on. But after it became clear that Will and I were mountain bike newbs, Gavin sped forward to try out some of the more expert obstacles.

"What'll you give me if I make the jump?" Will asks.

There's that light in his eyes again, the gleam that he had right before he kissed me last night. I stare at him for a long moment, then, "Nothing. Absolutely nothing."

He scowls at me and my gaze latches on to the fullness of his lower lip. Earlier, when I saw Gavin in shorts and a t-shirt, I waited for a flood of attraction, a flash of lust, something, anything...it didn't come.

But one look at Will and all I can think of is the look in his eyes when he pressed me against the wall and—

"Stop looking at me like that," he says in a low, husky voice.

I startle and shake myself out of the fantasy.

He moves his bike back and I maneuver off the path. Will picks up speed, hits the ramp perfectly and lands five feet past me. He brakes, turns around and gives me a wicked smile.

"Fine. You win. I'm the only one here who is terrible at mountain biking." I think for moment. "Or sports. I'm pretty terrible at all sports. Except walking."

Will smiles at me and I feel myself flush. "You're good at climbing trees."

"Is that a sport?"

"Obviously."

I smile and climb back on my bike. We start forward. Will lets me lead, since I'm the slower, more wobbly one.

"Looks like we lost Gavin." I check and am surprised that I don't feel disappointed.

"Not my doing," Will jokes. Then, "Is that okay?"

"I guess. I mean, he wanted to enjoy himself biking. He has to move faster than my snail pace if he wants to do that."

"I'm enjoying myself," Will says. "I like your snail pace."

I give a small smile that he can't see. I don't tell him, but I'm enjoying myself too. The mountain is beautiful in the summer. There are boulders and stony outcroppings covered in moss and ferns and the glistening of small natural springs leaking from the rocks. The smell of sun-warmed leaves and freshly biked-over dirt fills the air. A bird calling *zee-zee-zee* ascends in high notes.

"That's a warbler," I say. "Hear that call? They're common in New York. Prairie warblers, Canada warblers, chestnut sided warblers—"

"Wait," Will says. He pedals closer. "You really do go bird watching? With binoculars?" He sounds surprised and slightly embarrassed.

"Oh, so now you believe me? You think I really was birdwatching in the oak tree?"

I look back and grin. When he sees my smile, his expression shifts. "Nope. You're still a peeping Tom."

I look forward again. "We had a bunch of birdcall CDs at the library. I did a community program on New York birds one summer."

"Hence, warblers."

"Mhmm. They're funny birds. During courtship they perform dances in the air to show off their skills and chase after their chosen female." I don't know why I'm bringing up courtship with him.

"Fascinating."

I shiver at the way the word rolls off his tongue.

"They also sing to mark their territory and fight off other males."

"Hmmm. Do they?" There's a thoughtful note to his voice.

I carefully steer around a cluster of rocks. Gavin's tire tracks are on the trail, so he's still somewhere ahead of us. Maybe I should try harder to catch up with him.

"You didn't have to try very hard today," I say.

"Try what?"

"To separate me and Gavin."

There's a rickety-looking bridge, three wooden planks that are eight feet long, laid over a small rocky stream. I pull to a stop.

Will pulls up beside me. He steps off his bike. I look over in surprise. He lays it in the grass at the side of the trail.

"What are you doing?" I scoot my bike backwards.

"Trying harder," Will says.

A warm heat pools in my abdomen. It's a delicious melting feeling that says *yes*. That, more than anything else, scares me.

"I don't want to kiss you," I say, shaking my head.

His eyes flash in challenge.

I back my bike up a few more steps, then decide it's not fast enough, so I hop off and drop it to the grass. I back off the trail into the short woodland grass. Will follows. He unbuckles his helmet and drops it to the ground. I watch as he pulls off his bike gloves and drops them too.

My heart starts to flail like the beating of a bird's wings against my chest.

"Gavin, he's—" I cut off when Will reaches out and runs his fingers down my cheek.

An electric current runs through me, priming my body to receive his touch.

"Why were you working at three in the morning?" I ask, trying to distract him, or let's be honest, myself.

"I was on a call with the Tokyo office. Then later Dubai, then London." He's not really paying attention to what he's saying. Instead, his fingers trace along my jaw. I stand still, afraid to move, afraid not to. His fingers find the clasp of my helmet. He unbuckles it and slowly lifts the helmet from my head. Strands of hair fall around my face.

"You work too much," I say.

"Yes."

He takes my right hand and strokes the fabric of the bike glove.

"Why?" I ask.

He tugs at the fabric covering my pointer finger. It rides up, sliding to my knuckle. He wraps his fingers around my pointer and caresses my exposed skin and then firmly pulls until the tight fabric lifts off. He gently touches the tip of my finger and then moves to the next. He circles my middle finger, plays with it, then pulls the fabric up. Every tug, every touch, reverberates through me. Each time he pulls on a finger of my glove, I feel a responding tug low between my legs.

"Why do I work so hard?" he asks.

His voice is rougher than I've ever heard it. He moves to my ring finger and slides it through his hand. I gasp. The black of his pupils grows and nearly swallows his irises.

"Mhmmm," I say. I'm falling into a drunken lusty deliciousness where my body feels heavy and warm.

Will has removed my entire glove except for the pinky. He drags his hand over mine. I shiver at the feel of his heat covering me. He grabs the pinky and tugs. It comes off with no resistance. The glove falls to the grass.

I stare at my hand, naked and supple. Will threads his fingers through mine.

"Because that's what I do," he says.

Cold rushes over me. I hear the sardonic Will in his voice. He said the same thing the first time we kissed. I yank my hand from his. I stoop down and grab my glove and helmet.

"We should go."

Will reaches out. "Wait."

I turn back to him. I expect to see the cold, arrogant Will I've known so many years, and I startle when I realize he's not there. In fact, I don't think he's been there for some time. If I'm honest, years maybe. I think I've been seeing Will as he was in the past and not letting myself see him with fresh eyes. I guess that's the hard part about knowing someone so long and making judgments about them. You don't let them grow or change. In my mind, Will solidified as a villain at age eight and I never let him grow beyond that. But people change.

I look at Will.

His too-long hair falls across his forehead. He holds out his hand, his long fingers reach toward me. He looks like a mournful angel, beautiful, powerful, but unsure of whether or not he'll get what he's lost.

I wonder what he's lost.

I don't know. But I do know one thing, that maybe I'm finally seeing him in a new light. And I'm not so sure he's a villain. At least, I can give him the chance to begin again. Because the worst thing you can do to a person is freeze them in time and not let them move forward and grow.

"Yes?" I ask.

He drops his hand and steps towards me.

"Do you want to sit?" He gestures at the smooth short grass at the base of a mountain maple tree. I study him. Funny thing, if I don't assume that he has ulterior motives, I can almost believe that he's...thoughtful.

I sit in the grass and cross my legs. Will stretches out next to me.

"When I was nine, my dad realized that I was a mathematical prodigy."

I turn to look at him. I knew this, sort of. Everyone in Romeo heard about how Will was running the family's international accounting offices by age 14.

"He was proud?"

Will shakes his head no. "He hated it. I just wanted to play. Run around outside, climb trees, swim in the river, wrestle with my dog."

"You had a dog? I didn't think you liked dogs."

Will gives me a strange look. I try to imagine him with the puppy.

"My dad said he'd be damned if he'd stand by and watch me waste my talent. That he'd rather I'd never been born than to see me fritter away something he would've killed to have."

"What happened?" A cloud covers the sun and I feel cold. Will swallows and I catch him glancing at me from the corner of his eyes.

"He made certain I didn't waste my talent."

Something in his voice makes my heart crack. I think about the difference in him from age eight to age twelve. In four years he became so cold, so...

I reach out and put my hand on top of his.

He looks up in surprise.

"When my mom died," I begin, "I was eight. My dad cracked. He broke apart, and he was never able to put himself back together. Not even for me. He didn't speak more than a hundred words in nearly twenty years. Not even on the day he died. I told him I loved him and he...he said, 'Marlena.' That was my mom's name. And that was it. He died. So, I guess I'm saying, I don't know how it was with your dad, but I know how it feels to want a parent's love and not have it. I won't judge."

He shifts. Slowly he puts his arm around me and scoots me close.

"I fought him the first year. He banned play, toys, friends, video games, anything 'fun.' Anything outside of math and accounting that I showed an interest in, he removed." He says the word "removed" with a horrible finality.

"He didn't let you have friends?"

Will looks at me.

"No."

"How lonely."

Will shrugs.

"So that day when I asked you to be my friend and your dad came around the corner?" I ask.

Will gives a sharp nod and I ache to hold him.

"What about your dog?" Dogs are a boy's best friend.

"Riley was a distraction. He had him put down."

I stare at Will in mute horror. He doesn't look at me.

Finally he says, "I work because it's what I do. It's what I was trained to do and it's what I'm good at. It surprised the hell out of my dad when I became so good at it that I forced him out of business when I turned eighteen."

"Good," I say with vicious satisfaction.

Will gives me a small smile. "Then once he was out of my life, no longer pushing me, I realized I like what I do. I love it. He may have gone at it the wrong way, but he put me on the right path."

"I'm sorry."

"Don't be. I spent a few years as a teenager in therapy. It helped me realize I was angry with my father. I found the takeover of the company very cathartic."

He grins and I smile back.

But something's bothering me. "What about friends? Or hobbies or love? Don't you want those?" For years I never thought that Will had human enough emotions to desire those things, but now...I want him to have them.

Will turns toward me. I suddenly realize we're sitting close, our faces are inches apart. His arm is around my back. His fingers reach up and run through my loose hair. I shiver and my legs clench in response.

"Jessie?"

"Yes?"

"Can I please kiss you?"

I look into his eyes. They're wary and uncertain. I don't say anything for a moment. The cold, closed-off Will starts to reappear. I see him shifting his shield back in place.

"When we were fifteen," I begin.

His eyes narrow.

"Why did you really kiss me back?"

He lets out a harsh puff of air. He looks as if he's struggling with whether or not to tell me.

I run my fingers over his hand. He lets out another breath and when he looks at me again, his eyes have thawed.

"Because you were the closest thing to heaven I'd ever felt and I didn't want to stop."

My heart flips over in my chest. His lips curve into a small smile.

"You're not..." I pause, and clear my suddenly dry throat. "Why?"

"You've always been my friend," he says. "Even when you didn't know it."

"Yes," I say, and he understands.

He leans forward and takes my lips. I gasp as his mouth meets mine. He threads his hands through my hair and pulls me closer. He groans deep in his throat and the sound vibrates through me and reaches low down so that I lift my hips toward him.

He swears against my mouth, and I nip at his lips.

"You have no idea how much I want you," he breathes.

I reach up to stroke his shoulders. He grabs my wrists, leans me back to the grass and pins my arms over my head. He places his legs over mine, pinning me to the ground, and sets his mouth to mine.

I fall into the rhythm of his body rocking against me. His tongue strokes my mouth, his hips run over me and his length strokes my clit. I struggle in his grasp. I need my hands to pull off my shirt, to take off his. I want to touch him.

"Let me go," I say.

He pauses, then releases my hands. I smile and drag his shirt up over his chest. His eyes go dark with surprise, then want. I lean up and pull my shirt off, then my bra. My breasts bead and ache in the open air. Will lets out a hard breath and moves his hands to cup them. When his thumbs rub over my nipples, I gasp and arch toward him. His eyes spark like he's found a new hobby and he strokes me again. I cry out. He bends and pulls a nipple into his mouth. He grazes it with his teeth. I rock up against him. I send my hands over his muscular back, his shoulders. I tug at his hair as he teases my breasts with his mouth.

"Will."

He stops then. Goes completely still and quiet. Then he looks up at me and a strange light enters his eyes.

"Say that again," he demands.

"Will," I whisper, tasting his name on my tongue.

He grabs my mouth and kisses me hard and fast. I pull him to me and hold him close.

"Hey guys! Will. Jessie!"

I jerk up and fling my hands around my breasts. It's Gavin.

He's calling us and he's not far away. Will swears and grabs my T-shirt. He hands it to me and I thrust it over my head. I shove my bra in my pocket. Will moves just as fast. In seconds, we're both fully clothed and standing five feet apart. My heart hammers in my chest and I stare at Will.

What the heck did I just do?

Last night I could chalk up to a mistake, but today...I invited him to kiss me. I...wanted him to? Yeah, I did.

"Will? Jessie?" shouts Gavin.

I hear the snap of dry branches under bike tires.

"Over here," Will calls.

He glances at me, takes in my expression, my clenched hands and the fact that I can't hold his gaze.

"You have a twig," he says. He steps closer and reaches up to my hair.

Yes. I want his fingers threading through my hair. The realization makes me flinch. Will stiffens in response. Then he pulls the twig out and drops it to the ground.

He takes a good six steps back, and when I gather the courage to look at him again, all the warmth and yearning and openness is gone. His face is closed-off and expressionless and his stance is cold.

I want to go to him and tell him I didn't flinch because of him, but because I'm so confused. Because how can I feel these things for Will when Gavin is my soul mate?

"Will?" I look down the trail. Gavin is fifty feet away, just past the rickety log bridge.

"Yes?" His jaw clenches.

"I'm sorry," I whisper.

He shakes his head and looks away.

"Hey Jessie, watch this," shouts Gavin.

Will and I both turn to look. Gavin is at the bridge. He pulls up on his handlebars and the front tires leave the ground in an impressive wheelie. Then, he brings his front wheel down on the three logs. When he does, the logs split apart. There's a loud crack. Gavin yelps and tries to maneuver his bike.

I watch, completely stunned, as the bridge collapses and Gavin and his bike plunge into the rock-strewn water.

"Holy heck!" I shake off my shock and run toward the stream.

Will's faster. He reaches the stream and stands at the edge. Gavin lies in a pile of rocks, and the water rushes over him. His bike is tangled over his legs. He sputters and coughs.

"You okay?"

"Dang. Ahh. Dang." Gavin tries to sit up and falls back against the rocks. "I think I broke something."

"Huh," Will says. He wades into the water and assesses the situation. Based on the amount of swearing on Gavin's part and his level of pain, Will decides to call the paramedics. While he's on the phone, I take off my shoes and socks and climb into the cold stream. I squat down next to Gavin.

"Does it really hurt?"

Gavin grits his teeth. "It's not too bad."

I glance over at Will. He's talking to the 911 operator, but he's watching us from the corner of his eyes. Even now, he doesn't want to leave me alone with Gavin. I frown and look down at Gavin. He grimaces in pain and tries to put on a brave face.

Suddenly, I realize that once again fate has intervened just in time. I was confused and then Gavin fell. Gavin being injured is fate's way of letting me nurse him back to health. There are thousands of romance novels on the Florence Nightingale effect. Injured men falling in love with their nurses. I'll nurse him back to health and he'll finally feel that spark. And...so will I. All of my strategies didn't work, and that's because they weren't the right path to love.

I pat Gavin's hand. "Don't worry, the ambulance will be here in no time." I smile down at him and he gives a grateful smile back.

"Thank you," he says. "It helps having someone as pretty as you as a distraction."

I smile and ignore the pinch in my chest. I purposely don't look at Will as he splashes in the stream and pulls Gavin's bike to the grass. I don't look at him as he crowds close to me and checks on his brother. I don't...I can't look at him.

I feel like I'm betraying him, which is silly. Because fate couldn't have spoken any louder. It wants me to be with Gavin. It's paving the way for a classic Florence Nightingale romance.

It's basically a done deal.

11

WILL

TURNS out Gavin broke his coccyx, aka his tailbone. I spent twelve hours in the hospital with him and brought him back to the house with a doughnut pillow for him to sit on, and a load of prescriptions for pain. I slept for a few hours then woke at five to get some work done. There was a pile of emails from the lawyers concerning the merger with Duporte to review and the weekly numbers from my VPs to go over.

There was also a phone call from Alan Duporte concerning his and his wife's plans for the party this weekend. They'll be staying in Romeo and want to get together before the party. I notified my PA to book something. When I finished with everything it was already noon and I realized I hadn't eaten yet.

I walk down the back stairs to the kitchen. I can make a couple sandwiches, bring one to Gavin. See if he's awake yet. Then maybe I'll go find Jessie. I dreamed about her last night. She was in the oak tree and the branches were too high for me to reach her. I woke up frustrated and wanting her. It took twice as long to get the day's work done because I had to keep pulling my mind back from thinking about her.

I put four roast beef sandwiches together, grab a few dill pickles, two bottles of water, and put it all on a tray. My dad would have a fit if he saw me—the way I make my own meals, or wash my own dishes. He believed, firmly, that time is money, and any time spent doing menial tasks was robbing our family's bottom line. *That thirty minutes you just spent in the kitchen cost us $30,000*, he'd say. He's not wrong. In New York City, I have a chef, maid service, laundry service, a driver, a PA to take care of booking appointments and making reservations.

But here in Romeo, I like to leave all that behind.

I carry the tray down the hall toward Gavin's bedroom. He's in the east wing. It has darker wood trim, tall wainscoting and heavy curtains. I don't like this part of the house as much, maybe because it doesn't have as good a view of the meadow as the fourth floor. I make it to Gavin's room. His door is ajar. I pause at the entry.

The scene hits me in the gut and I exhale in surprise. Although I shouldn't be surprised.

Jessie sits on the edge of the bed. She has an open book next to her, and I swallow when I see that it's *The Horse and His Boy.* Soft light from the window falls on her and illuminates her like she's some sort of angel. I narrow my eyes. She's anything but.

She's wearing a white dress that stretches tight over her breasts and flares out around her hips. There are plates on the bed filled with half-eaten scones, berries, and cream. Two coffees with whipped cream and chocolate shavings in to-go cups from the bakery are on the nightstand.

"You don't read for fun? Not at all?" Jessie asks in surprise.

Neither of them has noticed me.

Gavin shakes his head. He looks a little wobbly, even reclining on a pile of pillows.

"Not at all." He beams at Jessie. I realize with shock that my brother is a little tipsy from the pain meds. "Although, if I'd had a librarian like you rather than old Mrs. Axham, maybe I would've learned to love reading."

Jessie smiles at him and I consider clearing my throat. Gavin's room is one of the smaller in the house. There's only space for a four-poster bed, a nightstand, a wardrobe, and a small desk that has a globe, a baseball, and a glove on top, all from childhood. He never liked Romeo and didn't bother to make this room his own. But the small size, the big bed and the soft light from the window make the setting intimate.

Gavin takes a strawberry and pops it in his mouth. "Will was the reader."

"Really?" Jessie asks.

Is that curiosity? I abort my plan to interrupt and step back from the doorway.

"He always had his nose in a book. When we were kids I'd catch him at midnight with a flashlight and a book. Had to warn him a few times our blasted father was coming."

"Why?" Jessie asks.

"Oh, he'd chuck Will's books in the trash."

I think I hear an angry choking noise from Jessie.

"Yeah," Gavin says. "The librarian, Mrs. Axham, hated Will. She thought he lost the books on purpose. Finally she got him banned from checking out books. So then, I checked them out for him and kept them in my room. I never read them though. I'm more the adventure type."

Jessie says something, but I can't hear it. Gavin laughs and I step toward the doorway.

"Why didn't we spend more time together?" Gavin asks. "You were here all these years. You're so nice. So fun. So friendly."

Alright, that's enough.

I step through the door and clear my throat. "I brought lunch."

Jessie looks up quickly and then pink blossoms in her cheeks.

"Gavin, you feeling better?"

Gavin smiles, "I feel great."

I step into the room and set the tray next to the coffee on the nightstand.

"Jessie came by to make sure I was okay. She's been keeping me company." Gavin gives her a dopey smile.

A tic starts in my forehead.

"You okay?" Gavin asks.

"Fine."

He tilts his head and studies me.

Jessie bunches the skirt of her dress in her hands and refuses to look at me.

Gavin lets out a long yawn and glances at Jessie. "I'm pretty tired. Maybe you'll read to me some more? I like it when you read to me."

I see red. If he weren't my brother and laid up with a broken tailbone, I'd put him in a headlock. I want to snatch up the book and take it back. I can't believe she's using the book I gave her to woo my brother.

"Scoot over," I say.

I land on the bed next to Gavin. The dishes rattle and he groans in pain at the jarring movement. Obviously he's not feeling that great. I grab a sandwich off the tray and take a bite. I chew and watch Jessie. She's staring at me like I might bite her. Her eyes narrow and her mouth purses.

"Of course I'll read more to you," she says sweetly, her voice dripping honey. That's when I know she's remembered that she's not backing down from her insane mission to win my brother's heart.

She opens the book and starts the chapter where Shasta meets Aravis. It's one of my favorite parts. The two of them shoot sparks off each other from the start. As Jessie reads, I finish off two sandwiches. I lean back against the headboard and start to relax. After the first page, Gavin falls asleep. Jessie doesn't notice, she keeps reading, her voice filled with warmth and enthusiasm. She even has different voices for each character.

I take the time to study her. She wore her hair down today, it falls around her face and almost softens the sharpness of her cheekbones and her eyes. Almost, but not quite. Which is good, because the sharpness of her chin and her cheeks and her arched eyebrows remind you of how stubborn she is. That stubbornness is her best and her worst feature. It's what helped her survive a childhood without love—the stubborn clinging to hope and the promise of the future full of love. But that stubbornness also makes her incapable of seeing what's right in front of her. Not just me wanting her. But that she has a whole community that loves her and considers her a member of their family.

Gavin lets out a long snore. Jessie looks up from her book.

"He's asleep," I say.

She frowns and sets her book down. "I'll go."

She reaches for the plates of scones and berries. She puts everything in a to-go basket from the bakery.

"I'll walk you out."

She bites her lip and then nods. I walk next to her down the dark hall to the front door. And I decide I don't want to walk her out, I want to keep walking with her—anywhere.

We reach the door. "What are you doing this afternoon?"

"Why?" Her brow furrows.

"Just wondering what you'll do with yourself since your merry nursemaid scheme was foiled."

She smirks at me. "Or was it?"

I have the urge to back her against the door and remind her of what we were doing yesterday. Her breath catches at my expression. She's going to run, I can tell. I have to think fast if I want her to stay.

"I need your help," I improvise.

"What?" She shakes her head.

"You were right. I need to learn more about this soul mate thing. Take me around town, introduce me to some couples. Help me understand."

She studies me, clearly skeptical. "You want me to help you understand soul mates?"

I nod.

"On one condition." She holds up a finger.

"Okay."

"If I convince you, you stop interfering in my love life."

She watches me and waits for my response. Finally, I hold out my hand. "Deal."

There's no way she'll ever convince me that this soul mate scheme is real and that she's meant for Gavin. No way on earth.

We shake on it.

12

JESSIE

WINNING this bet is going to be like taking candy from a baby. As soon as you start chatting with anyone in Romeo about love, they'll have a story to share about their brother or cousin or best friend who was matched by Miss Erma. It'll take a couple hours max to win this bet and get Will to leave me be. I frown and sneak a quick glance at him. To be honest, him letting me be isn't all that appealing.

He's in jeans and a Henley that stretches over his shoulders. He looks comfortable and hmm...happy? There's a shadow of dark stubble on his face and his hair is messy from what looks like a long night of combing his fingers through it while thinking. We're walking side-by-side down Main Street, and there's a looseness to his gait and a small smile on his lips. His smile is barely noticeable. Maybe it would be missed by anyone who doesn't know how to read his face and his subtle show of emotions.

"You like it here, don't you? You like Romeo," I ask, surprise in my voice.

"Why do you say that?" His stiff response doesn't fool me.

"I can't believe I never noticed before."

He gives me a sharp look. "Noticed what?"

"Gavin told me you own a penthouse in New York City, a place in London, an apartment in Tokyo, a villa in France, a beachfront home in the Caribbean, and—"

"Gavin was feeling talkative."

"He said, with all those houses, you choose to spend your weekends and free time in"—I hold my fingers to make air quotes—"'this boring, musty, empty old heap in the middle of nowhere.' The question is, why?"

I stop walking. Will slows and turns to face me.

"Why?" he asks, and I'm distracted by the blue of his eyes. They look like the chicory flowers that grow wild in the meadow. I smile. They're my favorite flower.

"It's because you like Romeo. Maybe even love it."

"Is that so?" He raises an eyebrow, and I hold back a smile.

I nod. "Sure. On the outside you're a businessman, one hundred percent, and people may think you have no time for things like love or a walk on a sunny afternoon." I gesture at Main Street, the sunshine, the flowers, the bright shops and the green park. "But we both know the people who think that way would be wrong."

"*We* do?" he emphasizes the word "we."

I nod and step closer to him, the hem of my dress brushing against his pant legs.

"Because, at heart, you're a romantic and a good man, and you come to Romeo because it's like you." The realization settles on me with surprising clarity. Who would've ever thought that I'd see these things in Will. "You're caring, hard-working, loyal, hope-filled. You come here more than anywhere else in the world because it feels like home. Your home."

Will gives me a look that's both skeptical and wary. "Are you trying to convince me that I already believe in Romeo's mythological soul mates?"

I tilt my head and look into his eyes, the skepticism wars against the wariness and wins.

"No," I say. "Maybe yes. No."

I look up at his full lower lip and try to block out the images of kissing him.

He draws in a sharp breath. I realize his pupils are dilating and starting to swallow the blue of his irises. I can see the memory of yesterday there. Will on top of me, in the grass.

"You forget," says Will in a low voice, "I've been coming here for twenty years but I don't talk to people. I don't know anyone. I don't go out and make friends or go to the town events. Your theory is flawed."

I shake my head. "You're a private person and an introvert. You don't have to go out to like someplace."

He raises his eyebrows and then lowers them. I can see his mind working.

"Gavin is extrovert. If a mosquito would have a conversation with him he'd chat back." I think about how much Gavin has talked the last two times we've been together. He's told me all about himself, and there's a few things that are very clear. One, he's a nice man. Two, we have absolutely nothing in common. And three, there's no spark. None.

"You're no extrovert. You're 'still waters run deep'. It's not that you don't like people, it just takes you a while to warm up."

Will gives me a smile. "So, you don't still think I have a calculator for a heart?"

Mortification washes over me. I was such a judgmental jerk. "No. I'm sorry."

"Looks like you have me all figured out." His lips quirk into a smile and I realize he's laughing at me.

"Fine. Maybe not. But I do think you'll admit by the end of the day that I'm right."

"Not a chance," he says.

I step back and shake out my skirt. I'm trying, unsuccessfully, to shake off the magnetic attraction I feel for Will.

"Come on then. First stop." I cross the street to Miss Lydia's Dance Studio.

IF ANYONE CAN CONVINCE WILL THAT SOUL MATES ARE REAL, IT'S Miss Lydia. She's seventy years old, as fit and spunky as a twenty-five-year-old, and she's taught half the wedded couples in town their wedding dance.

"Jessie, congratulations!" she cries when Will and I step into the studio. "I heard Erma saw your soul mate."

She steps away from the ballet barre and rushes toward us. She's in a leotard and tights. Her mom and tots ballet class is in thirty minutes. Lydia stops in front of us and looks Will up and down.

"Hmm. You'll do. You're a lucky man, Jessie takes care of all the strays, castaways, and lonely folk. Her library programs help so many. If you hurt her, we'll form a mob and tear you to pieces." Lydia ends in a serious tone at odds with the sweet smile on her face.

I choke on a cough. She thinks Will is my soul mate and she's threatening him.

"No, he's—"

"I won't hurt her," Will says a solemn voice.

I look over at him. He holds up his hand like he's on the witness stand.

"I solemnly swear," he says.

Lydia stares at him a moment and then starts to cackle. "I like this one. He's got chutzpah, Jessie. I always thought you'd do well with chutzpah. No namby-pamby for you."

"But—" I start, but Will moves over and steps on my toe. I squeak. "Hey!"

"What's that?" Lydia asks.

"I was going to say, he's not—"

"A good dancer. Or informed on soul mates. Jessie said you know all about Romeo's soul mates."

Lydia smiles and waves her hands in front of her in some sort of elegant dance gesture. "I do. I can tell you all about it while I assess your dancing."

"Perfect," Will says.

I frown at him. "Why are you letting her believe you're my soul mate?" I whisper.

He leans close and whispers back, "Why are you believing I'm not?"

My mind goes blank. I stop and stare at him. Lydia claps her hands and I come back to the moment.

"Come to the dance floor," she says.

Will strides out. I follow him, but I'm hesitant and skittish. I'm not certain what he's going to say or do next.

His soul mate?

No.

Except... No.

I haven't loved him my whole life. In fact, I've only started to like him in the past few days. Erma specifically said my soul mate was the Williams boy I'd loved since I was a kid. That I knew who he was.

"Erma's never wrong, right, Lydia?" I ask.

"That's right." She skillfully pushes Will and me together and places our hands in the proper positions.

Will's right hand feels warm and heavy on my left shoulder

blade. He spreads his hand across my bare back and a liquid warmth flows over me. My whole body, all my senses and awareness are focused on the spot where his fingers press against my skin. He takes his left hand and clasps my right. His grip is gentle, with a quiet strength. He runs his thumb over the back of my hand, so featherlight that I'd miss it if I weren't so aware of him.

The stroke of his fingers on my hand vibrates over me all the way down to my core. I clench my legs together and try to stay in the here and now. We're in Lydia's studio to talk about soul mates.

Soul mates.

I put my other hand on Will's right shoulder. My mouth goes dry and I hold back an involuntary sound of pleasure. The right side of his lips turns up in a half-smile. He *knows*.

I try to get a grip. But my body keeps reminding me that the last time I gripped Will's shoulders, he had me against a wall, or on the ground. With his mouth on me. I let out a sharp pant.

"Perfect," Lydia says. "I can always tell whether a couple will make it. Erma has her soul mate predictions, but I have dance."

Will looks into my eyes. "Really?"

"Try this," Lydia says. "We'll do some basic waltz steps." She demonstrates, and Will leads me in a languid movement.

Lydia continues. "Dancing with your partner is the best way to learn their secrets. You can learn in ten minutes flat what they'll be like in marriage and whether or not you fit."

I want to say something, but my tongue is sticking to the roof of my mouth and Will's hand has short-circuited the wires between my tongue and my brain.

"That's interesting," Will says. I can't tell if he's talking to Lydia or commenting on the way I'm melting into him.

As Will flows into another waltz move, Lydia goes on. "More than interesting. Listen close. Sure, you can tell if a man will be good in bed by how he dances, the way he leads you, if he responds to you, your chemistry."

Will spins me in a turn and pulls me back to him. My breath catches at the look in his eyes. *I'll always want you,* he said. A week ago, heck, three days ago, I would've thought he was lying or had an agenda. But now...I'm not so sure. I think I could believe him. Which scares me.

"But there's more," Lydia says. "Dance, like marriage, is a partnership. Cooperation is key. If either dance partner showboats, or doesn't respect the other, or refuses to compromise, or dislikes looking foolish, or doesn't acknowledge the other's feelings or respond to them, or isn't respectful or honest with the other in how they want to "dance"—all those problems will come out in marriage. People could save themselves heartache and breakups by signing up for a dance lesson and seeing how they mesh on the dance floor. In ten minutes I can tell you what fifty years of marriage will look like."

Will squeezes my hand and my heart lurches. But when I look at him, his face is inscrutable. Maybe I imagined it.

"So, how are we doing?" Will asks.

Lydia circles around us. I can't bring myself to say anything, to tell Lydia that Will isn't my soul mate.

I'll always want you.

I look back at us in the studio mirror along the back wall. Will holds me tenderly, closely. He holds me as if he...cherishes me. His stance is open, vulnerable, like he trusts me. I grip his shoulders and look up at him. His lips twitch and there's a hint of humor in his eyes.

"You'll do," says Lydia. "Your personalities go well together. There's attraction. Sexual compatibility."

I cough and Will pats my back. The corners of his eyes

crinkle and I get the feeling he's laughing again without actually laughing. How did I miss this before?

"The only trouble I foresee from your dancing is openness. Your stance is slightly guarded. You'll have to open up fully, be honest, trust. La," she trills, "you'll get there. Miss Erma is never wrong." She waves her hands and gestures at us.

I still stand in Will's arms even though we've stopped dancing. I clear my throat and slowly step back. Will's hand falls from my back and he slowly lets my hand go. My whole body vibrates with prickly warmth and it's begging me to step back in Will's arms and start dancing again.

I watch as Will swallows. His Adam's apple visibly bobs. He glances at me, then away. There's a heavy tension between us and it looks as if he's visibly stopping himself from taking me in his arms.

I pull in a steadying breath. "What about soul mates?" I ask, remembering our reason for coming. "Will doesn't know about soul mates."

Lydia smiles and her wrinkles soften. "Erma predicted my marriage with Anthony. More than forty years now. She saw it while he was still fighting in Vietnam. He came back, missing both legs, touchy as a bear roused early from hibernation. For five years we fought Erma's prediction. He wouldn't dance with me."

Will nods. "That's hard."

"It was. But finally, we both got our heads and hearts straight. He danced with me, and that was it. Six kids, seven grandkids, and more than forty years later, I'm more in love than ever. I'm thankful Erma saw my soul mate in Anthony. He's the only dance partner I can imagine spending my life with."

"So you believe in the soul mate predictions?" Will asks.

Lydia waves her arms. "Me and the two hundred and seven

couples I taught wedding dances to. You'll be number two hundred and eight." She winks at us.

Oh no.

"Lydia, thank you, but you misunderstood—"

"Tut, tut. I won't hear it. You two are naturals. Lessons from me or I'll be terribly offended."

"No, I mean were not—"

The door swings open and half a dozen two and three-year-olds run into the studio, squealing and stomping, their moms trailing behind. Our time is up. Lydia waves goodbye as the toddlers surround her.

"So, are you convinced yet?" I ask Will when we're on the sidewalk. "About Erma's predictions," I clarify.

He leans his head back and lets the sun bathe his face with light. When he looks back at me, his gaze is thoughtful.

"If I say yes, you'll hold me to our bet? I have to stay out of your love life?"

My stomach turns over, like it's falling out of the old oak tree.

"Yes," I say, and my stomach feels like it hits the ground.

Will shrugs. "Then no. I'm not convinced."

His words from the studio hang between us.

Why do you believe I'm not your soul mate?

13

WILL

"I HAVE A QUESTION," says Jessie.

"Alright."

We're leaving the hardware store, where Mr. and Mrs. Kwan told us how their son found his soul mate because of Erma. They're ecstatic to finally have grandchildren. Before that, we stopped to chat with the town sheriff. He was grabbing a coffee and told us about his match almost twenty years ago. The gruff and hardened sheriff wanted me to understand that Miss Erma's word was akin to the law. And also, that this town made certain Erma wasn't bothered by newspapers, journalists, cuckoo birds, crazy love seekers, or general nuisances.

"You're still not a believer? Even after the Kwans and Sheriff Rodham?"

"I'm not convinced." If I believe in this, it means I'll have to keep my word, leave her alone and watch her marry my brother. "Was that your question?"

The breeze ruffles her hair and she pushes it out of her eyes.

"No."

She studies me and I stand still and let her look me over and work out whatever she's pondering. She starts walking down the sidewalk and I fall in beside her.

"All those years," she begins, then stops.

I nod. "Yeah?"

She chews he bottom lip, then, "All those years, when I saw you around town, I'd smile at you and you'd never smile back, you'd just turn away."

There's a bitter taste in my mouth. I realize it's guilt and regret.

"That's true."

She'd smiled at me from the time I was seventeen and until the day after I turned twenty-one. Gavin and I had our twenty-first birthday in Romeo. I'd just fought off my father's second takeover attempt since ousting him from the company. I was in a hell of a mood and Gavin was ready to party. We'd gone and spent the night at the bar—the one and only time I've ever gone on a bender. Gavin went home with a tourist looking for romance in the Town of Love. Not me. For some reason, I stumbled out of the bar at four a.m. and fell asleep on the bench outside the library.

Jessie shook me awake three hours later. She was returning a pile of books to the book drop. When I opened my eyes, the sun felt like a knife prying open my skull.

"Will? Are you okay?" she'd asked.

And because I felt like I was going to die by hangover, it was only natural that she looked like an angel. She gave me that slow, cautious smile and I closed my eyes to block it out.

"Should I call someone? Gavin?" The way she said "Gavin," breathless and worshiping, sent a howling jealousy through me. Gavin was likely in bed on round number six with his birthday girlfriend and here Jessie was, the woman I'd always wanted, here she was, wanting Gavin.

"What can I do to help?" she asked.

Kiss me, want me, I ached to say. But I was bruised and sore from another corporate battle with my father. And the world's worst hangover and a six-year-long hard-on for this woman, the one who doesn't want me, made me say bitterly, "You can help by leaving me the hell alone."

She gasped and I grew angry at my inability to do such a simple thing as be charming.

"I'm not Gavin," I added viciously. "So stop smiling at me." She may smile at me, but she beamed at Gavin.

I got my birthday wish. In the years since, Jessie never smiled at me again. I'd loved her smiles. I'd hated her smiles. But I hated it even more when the smiles stopped.

I look over at Jessie and I'm pulled back into the present.

"Why?" she asks. "After your dad was gone and you were in charge of your life, why didn't you ever smile at me, or say something nice or tell me..." She fades off and her cheeks turn pink.

We're near the river and the stone footbridge. She stops and picks a dangling leaf from a nearby maple tree and tosses it into the river. The leaf floats on top of the swirling water and is carried downstream under the bridge. I watch until it's out of sight around the bend.

"Did you ever notice that people stay in situations that are uncomfortable or intolerable? They stay and don't try to leave or change. Do you ever wonder why?" I ask.

We move to the grassy edge of the sloping riverbank. The grass curls over into the water and the sun shines golden on the rippling water. A cool breeze comes off the shallow sun-dappled river.

Jessie sighs. "It seems safer to stay with what you know than leave and risk something worse. It's why I never yelled at my dad or demanded that he talk to me. Because what if he said something I didn't want to hear? Like he didn't want me. Or didn't love me. Silence, as horrible as it was, was better than risking what I was afraid he might say."

I look over at her downturned face. The sun and shadow play over her bare shoulders and the white lace of her dress. I reach over and tuck a loose strand of hair behind her ear. "You're loved," I say.

She looks up with wide, shocked eyes.

I smile ruefully. "Look around this town. People light up when they see you coming. The kids love your library story time. The seniors at the retirement home love your visits and book bundles. I've had a dozen people stop me and tell me how you brought them books when they were sick and housebound, or helped with their résumé, or helped them learn to do a dozen different things. Half this town is in love with you."

She laughs and brushes my words aside.

We're silent for a moment, watching the river pass. Her hand dangles next to mine and I ache to reach out and grab it.

"You know why I never smiled at you, never tried to change?"

She looks at me. "Why?"

"At first I wanted to protect you. Then I wanted to protect myself. I knew how you felt about me. Over the years we made a pattern of how we interacted and the roles we played. I didn't know how to stop. It felt better to be in an intolerable situation with you than in any situation without."

A small wrinkle forms between her eyebrows.

"Will..." She reaches out to put her hand on my arm.

"I was afraid that if I tried to change things, that you'd..."

"The risk was worse than the silence," she says.

I swallow and nod. "That's right."

"What changed?" She takes her hand off my arm. I watch as she crosses her arms over her chest.

"Things staying the same became infinitely worse than risking rejection." I glance at her then down at my hands.

"Because Erma said Gavin is my soul mate."

I look back at her. "No. Because I don't want to imagine the rest my life without you in it. Also, he's not your soul mate."

She shifts from one foot to another, then looks at me with her brows lowered.

"What will you do if it's proved he is?"

My chest tightens painfully, but I smile through it. "I'll turn Gothic villain. I'll kidnap you and keep you locked up in my mansion where I'll pamper you and give you everything you could ever desire. Books by the thousands, first editions, autographed copies, rare manuscripts. Thirteenth century love poems. I'll make you mochas with the extra chocolate you always want but never ever ask for. I'll fill closets with vintage dresses procured from around the world. I'll give you heaven on a platter."

Her eyes are wide and slightly glazed, just how they look right before I kiss her.

"There's only one catch," I say. "Heaven comes with me, soul mate or not."

Her eyes clear and she nods. "Right. I uh, I had another stop. Hart's Chocolates? We should go before they close. I still have to convince you soul mates are real."

I look again at the river, a leaf flows past, unable to break free from the current.

"Alright," I say. There's a hollowness expanding in my chest. Jessie walks to the footbridge and I step next to her.

"Will?" she turns to me.

I raise my eyebrows in response. "Hmm?"

"I wish..." She shakes her head. Then, "I wish we'd become friends sooner."

I don't know what she was going to say before she cut off, but I know that wasn't it. I don't remind her of what I said before—that she's always been my friend.

～

"AND THAT," SAYS GREGORY HART, "IS HOW ERMA LED ME TO THE love of my life."

Jessie and I are in the chocolate tasting room at Hart's Chocolates. Gregory, a stout fifty-year-old with a handlebar mustache, pinches his wife Martina on her bottom. She smacks him with her kitchen towel. She's not quite five feet tall. She has wide brown eyes, streaks of gray in her hair and an infectious smile.

The smell of rich chocolate fills the air. The shop reminds me of the inside of a chocolate box. It's painted in dark brown, red, and gold. The walls are lined with hot cocoa mixes, foil-wrapped chocolates, and candies. On the far wall there's a glass case full of freshly made truffles and things like chocolate-covered orange peel and chocolate-coated toffee. As soon as we walked in, my mouth started to water.

Jessie and I are seated at a small tasting table near the back of the store. There are a few marble-topped tables with café chairs, secluded from the rest of the shop where customers can sit and have chocolate and coffee in private.

Since Jessie and I are the only ones in the store, Gregory and Martina were more than happy to share the story of their soul mate connection.

"When Erma said to Gregory he'd find his love on the cocoa farm in Peru where he bought his beans, he flew down and spent six months in the village convincing me to marry him," Martina says.

Martina and Gregory share a look and then she laughs and smacks him again with her towel.

"How did you convince Martina she was your soul mate?" asks Jessie.

"With chocolate, of course," Gregory says.

Martina laughs and smiles her wide infectious grin and Gregory turns bright red.

"You're fated, no? I can see it," Martina says.

"No," Jessie says.

"Yes," I say at the same time.

Martina doesn't hear either of us. She's walked over to the truffles and ducked below the counter into the chocolate case. She's pulled on white cotton gloves and has a delicate white china plate. Gregory brings over two cups of water and two long white scarves.

"We're going to give you a demonstration of how chocolate and love are alike. You'll be our guinea pigs for the new class we want to teach," Gregory says.

Martina has lined six truffles on the plate, two each of three different varieties.

"You're going to have a blind tasting," explains Gregory. "Put on the blindfolds, feed each other the chocolates, and take turns saying what you taste. You can describe texture, flavor, memory, emotion, a sensation."

I look over at Jessie and a bright pink blush travels across her cheeks.

"I'm sorry, Gregory, but Will and I aren't together," Jessie says.

"Yet." Gregory winks.

The bell at the front of the store rings, announcing a customer.

"We'll be at the front. Enjoy," Martina says. She and Gregory hurry to greet the customer. Gregory sneaks in another pinch and Martina smacks him with her towel. I wonder how many times in the past twenty-five years they've reenacted that pinch and whack.

Jessie clears her throat. "We don't have to do this if—"

"Of course we do. You're teaching me about true love and soul mates. It's part of the lesson."

She purses her lips, but her eyes flicker to the truffles. All six are glossy dark chocolate, rectangular and plump, their flavors hidden beneath the chocolate shell.

"I know you want to," I say. "And you don't want to disappoint the Harts. Plus, maybe this time I'll be convinced. But the only way that'll happen is if we feed each other the chocolate."

I hold up the long silk scarf. Jessie's eyes cloud over. I feel like we're in the Garden of Eden and I'm offering her the forbidden fruit. Perhaps it wasn't an apple or a pomegranate, but cocoa.

She eyes the scarf like it's a snake, but she leans towards me. "Fine. Yes. We'll do it."

I smile, feeling elated.

"Together," she says. She lifts the second scarf.

I swallow, my throat suddenly dry. I reach for the glass of water and take a long drink. Then I set the glass back on the white marble. I lean forward in my chair and move the three matching chocolates to opposite sides of the plate.

"Top first. Then middle, then bottom," Jessie says.

I nod. For some reason, I feel like I'm fifteen and we're on our first date. A date before she kissed me and said Gavin's name. Before I ruined any good feeling she might have for me.

My hands shake as I lift the scarf. Her eyes are solemn and watchful. I try to give her a small smile but I can't make my lips turn up.

I steady my shaking hands as I wrap the white scarf over her eyes and tie it in place at the back of her head. My fingers brush her silky soft hair and I imagine what it would feel like to run my hands through it as she lays under me on my white bedsheets. I pull the knot tight and run my fingers over the scarf, tracing her cheeks, making sure it's secure. Her lips are a contrasting bright red against the white fabric. The tip of her tongue darts out and she wets her lips. She has no idea how erotic she looks.

"All good? You can't see?" I manage to say. I take a deep breath of the chocolate-scented air.

"No, I can't see." She holds up the scarf in her hand. "Your turn."

I lean toward her. She reaches out and feels the air between us. Her hands land on my chest. She pulls away, then softly places them on my face. Her fingers drift gently over my skin. She lingers for a moment longer than necessary, and I watch as she draws in a nervous breath. Then she wraps the scarf over my eyes and pulls the fabric tight.

"Can you see?"

"Nothing." The world is now a grayish blank canvas behind the scarf. My view of Jessie is gone. But I can still feel her next to me. The pull between us is there, even when I can't see her.

"Ready?" I ask.

I reach for the plate and pick up the first truffle. I hear her do the same.

"Ready."

I reach out and find her lips. I hold the chocolate to her

mouth. She opens and carefully wraps her lips around my fingers and the chocolate. She pulls it free, running her teeth over my skin. I shiver at the sensation. She lets out a quiet sound of pleasure.

Then it's my turn. She holds the chocolate against my lips and rubs it over my bottom lip. I take it from her hand, softly as a gentle kiss. The dark chocolate flavor explodes in my mouth. I bite into it.

It's chilies. Chilies and dark chocolate ganache.

Jessie shifts next to me and I hear her let out a soft breath.

"Heat," she says.

"Passion," I say.

"Complexity," she says in a careful, neutral voice.

"Longing," I say.

I hear her grab her glass of water and take a long swallow. "Let's try the next," she says, ignoring my descriptions.

I take a drink to clear the flavor of spiced, heated longing, and reach for the next chocolate.

When I hold the truffle out to her, she takes it with a perfunctory, impersonal bite. I follow her lead and take the chocolate from her fingers with my teeth. The flavors are dark chocolate, bergamot and black tea. They coat my tongue and fill me with a nostalgic warmth.

"Tea," she says.

I smile. "When you first gave me *The Horse and His Boy* and I read the Narnia series, I imagined having tea just like they did. Strong and piping hot, at a table with all your friends. I imagined having tea with you too. I was twelve, we talked about books and drank hot tea. In my mind, it tasted just like this."

The flavor of warm tea lingers on my tongue. I smile at the memory of my twelve-year-old-self wanting to have tea with Jessie.

"What did we say at your imaginary tea party?" Her voice is soft and there's a whisper of curiosity and connection.

I haven't thought about those imaginings in years. I never lingered on things I knew couldn't come true.

"At first, we talked about what books we were reading. When I told you The *Voyage of the Dawn Treader* was my favorite book, you made a compelling argument that brought me back over to *The Horse and His Boy*."

"Did I?" she asks, a smile in her voice. Then, "What did you like about *The Voyage of the Dawn Treader*?"

I pause, afraid to tell her. But she leans closer to me and her leg presses against mine. I wait, count to five, but she doesn't pull away.

I begin, "Because Eustace is a horrid, miserable character that no one likes—"

"Rightly so."

"Rightly so," I agree. "But then he hits rock bottom and sees how wrong he's been. He asks forgiveness and he's given it." My voice is quiet and I can hear the plea in it, although I don't know if Jessie can.

"Redemption," she says. She reaches over and finds my hand, then threads her fingers through mine.

"I'm sorry," I whisper. I pause for a moment and feel the warmth of her hand in mine.

She squeezes my hand. "What did we talk about after books?"

I shrug even though she can't see me. "I was twelve. I told you about how hard things were. In my imagining you were very understanding." I smile even though she can't see me.

"It's funny. When I was that age, I'd sit in the oak tree and read and look at your house."

"Look for Gavin" goes unsaid.

"I've come to the conclusion that reality is always better than fantasy," I say.

She's silent a moment, then she says, "Hmm. I think you're right."

"Should we try the last one?"

"Let's."

She keeps her left hand laced in mine and reaches for the chocolate with her other hand. Slowly, she places the truffle against my lips. When I take it, she rubs her thumb across my lower lip and lets her fingers linger there. I close my eyes behind the blindfold and memorize her touch.

She pulls back. The chocolate melts over my tongue and the flavors slowly unfold. I sigh in recognition.

I take the last chocolate from the plate and hold it up for Jessie. When she takes it, I press my second finger against her lips in the replica of a kiss.

"Red wine," she says.

It's dark chocolate with a red wine infusion, and the wine is tinted with the flavor of the wine barrel.

"Oak," I say.

"Oak," she agrees.

"Friendship," I say.

"First kiss," she whispers.

"First kiss," I agree.

"Wanting and wishing," she continues. "A lifetime's worth of wanting and wishing."

I stiffen and slowly pull my hand from hers. We've been wanting and wishing for two different things. I take the scarf from my eyes and blink at the bright light. Jessie pulls the scarf off and blinks at me. Her cheeks are pink and her eyes have changed. She isn't looking at me in the same way.

I push the chair back and stand up.

"I still don't believe in soul mates," I say stiffly. "I won't leave you be. I won't admit you're meant for Gavin."

She nods and smooths her hands over her white skirt. "I know. Do you mind if we have one more stop tonight?"

She's completely composed, while I'm the exact opposite.

I look at my watch. It's nearly seven. "Alright."

"Good. I think this one will do the trick. There's no way you won't believe after this."

I shake my head. Not a chance.

14

JESSIE

THE LIBRARY CLOSED AT FIVE. The lights are low and the building is silent. I lead Will through the rows of nonfiction toward the back of the building. The sound of our footsteps is muted on the carpet and I can hear Will's soft breath from behind me.

He hasn't said anything since walking the two blocks from Hart's Chocolates to the library. He didn't even say anything when I opened the back door of the closed and dark library. It's because he's said everything that needs to be said. He wants me, he always has. He won't step aside and acknowledge Erma is right about my soul mate. There's nothing more for him to say. The move is mine.

I stop at the end of a row of books. There's a large thick wooden table with ten upholstered chairs placed around it. The table is handmade and carved around the edges is a scrolling pattern of leaves, branches and acorns. The walls are painted with a mural of an oak tree. Its branches are filled with books. I had the painting commissioned five years ago, shortly after I started working here and was placed in charge of updating the reference section. Will steps beside me. He looks at the mural and lets out a long sigh.

"I didn't know this was here," he says.

My breath catches at the quiet awe in his voice. "I had it painted after I started working here."

He steps to it and runs his hands over the titles of all the books in the tree. His hand stops at the heart of the tree, where I put my favorite. When he turns to me, his expression is hungry.

"Is this what you wanted to show me?"

I move toward him, drawn in by the hunger in his gaze.

"No," I say.

I take another step toward him. Even when I wanted to, I could never stay away from him. Even now, when Erma told me my dream had finally come true and Gavin is my soul mate, I can't stay away from Will.

"Then what did you want me to see?"

He looks down at my lips and I imagine him tasting me, tasting the memory of oaky chocolate and hot tea. Of friendship, and dreams, and first kisses and wishes.

I take a deep breath and turn to the tall bookcase with the locked glass door. Inside are all the reference books, the books with leather bindings and gold leaf edges. I take out my key ring and insert a small gold key into the lock. The glass door clicks open. I pull out a thick well-worn album and hold it to my chest.

"This is one of two albums in Romeo that records every soul mate match since 1948." Chloe has the other album. It's kept by her Aunt Erma. I set the heavy book on the table. "The head librarian has always been in charge of keeping the records."

"I see. It's your irrefutable proof." He gives me a wry smile.

I sit down in one of the cushioned chairs at the table and open the book to the last page. It's a picture and record of Veronica's wedding.

Will sits down in the chair next to me. He turns the pages and we look at the pictures. The styles of the wedding dresses and tuxedoes change as we flip back through the decades, until we're at a photo of a man in a World War II era Air Force uniform kissing his bride.

I stop looking at the pictures and instead I watch Will. When he leans down, a lock of hair falls across his forehead. I want to reach out and brush it back. As he looks through the pages, his fingers curl under with tension. I ache to take his hand. Will reaches the last page and gently closes the book. We sit in the quiet stillness of the library. Neither of us speaks.

Finally, I run my hand over the soft leather binding. "I used to wish that someday I'd end up in this book."

Will nods, a short, curt acknowledgment.

"And now that Erma saw my soul mate, I could be the next entry."

Will's jaw clenches. I reach out and brush my fingers along it. He looks at me. His body coils with tension but he doesn't move.

"Do you know what I realized?" I don't take my hand from his cheek.

"What?" he says, his voice is raw.

"You were right. It doesn't matter anymore."

Will swallows and his eyes narrow on me. "What does that mean?"

I take my hand off his cheek. "Erma said that my soul mate was the Williams boy I've always loved. But I loved a fantasy. I loved the idea of Gavin. I hung onto that fantasy for years, it was the life raft that got me through the worst storm of my life.

But I'm on dry land now. I don't need a fantasy anymore. It's time I admitted I loved the idea of a person, not the actual person."

Maybe Erma did make her first mistake. Because there's nothing between Gavin and me, not even the smallest spark. The only thing Gavin and I have common is…Will.

I look at Will and give him a small smile. "You don't have to keep hanging around, sticking to me like glue. Your brother is safe. Your business merger is safe."

Will stares at me, then his expression shifts from confused to stunned to determined.

"I believe in soul mates," he says.

"What?" I shake my head. What is he talking about?

"I believe in soul mates," he says more firmly. He gestures at the book, "I believe in them."

"What? Why?" I push away from the table so I can see him better. Why is he admitting this now?

"Because the first time I saw you I knew I wanted to be yours for the rest of my life."

I think about him pushing me into the mud puddle. "You didn't."

"I did," he says firmly. "And every time I saw you after that, the feeling only grew stronger. If that isn't a belief in soul mates, I don't know what is."

A warmth flows through me and I realize something. "You've been the one constant in my life. You've been with me for the last twenty years. I know more about you than I do about anyone else."

It's true. And I'm no longer surprised that it's true. Every time Will came to town, I vibrated at his presence like a tuning fork freshly struck. All those years I "disliked" him, I was aware of him, fighting my desire, fighting that he was the one. My one.

"Can I be honest?"

His eyes warm and he nods.

I clasp my hands together and drop them in my lap. Then I whisper, "I'm terrified that if I tell you I want you—"

He lets out a harsh breath. I pause but he doesn't say anything, so I continue.

"If I tell you that I want you, I'm terrified you'll stand up, smiled coldly, and walk away. But not before you let me know that I should've realized you'd do anything to keep me from ruining your business and your brother's life. I'm terrified the second I admit how I feel, you'll let me know this was all a game. And you'll leave me." I look down at my clasped hands. I'm afraid to look in his face. "I'm scared because I don't care about being in this book anymore. I don't care about soul mate predictions or fate. I just care about you."

He pushes back from the table and my stomach drops. I hold my breath, waiting for him to say something, anything.

He steps next to me and holds out his hand, palm up. I let out my held breath and slowly place my hand in his. The touch of his skin on mine sends a whispered promise through me. He pulls me to my feet. We stand facing each other. Cool, muted light and thousands of books surround us. He takes my other hand and squeezes gently.

"Tell me," he says. His eyes warm to the shade of the blue chicory flowers I love. The ones from my meadow.

"Say it," he whispers.

My heart beats so hard against my rib cage that my chest hurts. I've never admitted to anyone, not my dad or my friends, not anyone, that I want them or need them. Because then they might leave me.

Will looks down at me and squeezes my hands again.

My chest feels like it's being hammered down by my

pounding heart. I stare into Will's eyes and grab onto the familiarity of them like a lifeline.

"I want you," I say. "I need you."

Will lets out a low sound and lets go of my hands. Instead of walking away he pulls me to him. His eyes fill with need.

"I'm going to kiss you."

"Yes."

Then he takes my face in his hands, runs his fingers in my hair and lifts my lips to his. He lets out a possessive noise and I catch the sound in my mouth. I didn't know it, but every kiss before this has been restrained. Will pours his need into my mouth, I catch it, suck on his tongue, lick his lips.

He pulls me closer. His fingers trail through my hair, grasp me tight. He takes one arm and lifts me onto him. I wrap my legs around his hips. My breasts rub against his chest and it sends a throb between my legs. I sink into him, and when I feel the hard length of him pressed against me, I gasp. He puts his hand to my lower back and presses me closer. I cry out and rock into him. His tongue thrusts in and out of my mouth mimicking the movement of my hips.

"Will," I cry out. Little electric sparks pulse through me and travel down to the space between my legs.

"Say it again," he whispers against my mouth.

"I want you."

He carries me backwards until my back hits the bookcase against the wall. Books tumble around us and hit the floor. He steps to the side and presses me to the wall. He sends his mouth to my throat and sucks on my pulse point. I cry out and grab the edge of the shelf, knocking more books off. He swears and his hands squeeze my hips and pull me closer. My dress flares up and over my hips. There's nothing separating us but my panties and his jeans. I arch into him and he bucks.

"What else?" he asks. "Tell me what else."

I know what he's asking for.

"I need you," I whisper. "I need you."

His eyes fill with wild joy. He kisses me, swings me around and sets me gently to the floor. I shove the books aside. He lowers himself on top of me, his legs nestle around mine, his arms cage me in. He looks down at me, there's the joy I saw, and something else, something that makes my heart pound.

I think it's...love.

I recognize it because I feel the same thing. There's no running from it, not here, not now.

I can see it in his eyes, he's not going to leave me, not ever. Like he said, he'll give me heaven, soul mate or not. I'm not afraid anymore. He's mine and I'm his.

"I want you," I say. His eyes go dark.

He runs his hands over my ribs and sends his thumbs to circle my nipples. I cry out and lift my hips and press them against him.

"If we do this. You're mine. I'm not letting you go." He says it as a warning.

"Promise?"

He grins then flips up my dress and slides my panties down my legs.

"Promise," he says. Then he drops his mouth to my clit. He sucks on me and I cry out at the flood of sensation. I grab his shoulders. He moves his hands to my bare thighs and holds me in place as he strokes me with his tongue.

A fiery heat consumes me, fills me, and I want more. I want Will. I drag my fingers over his shoulders, up his cheeks, through his hair. He hums on my clit and it throbs in response. I arch up to him and he grabs my hips and holds me against his mouth. I'm in his arms, bare to him, open.

"Cum for me," he says.

The fire grows hotter, I'm drunk on it. There's only the heat, me and Will.

"Cum for me," he demands.

He flicks his tongue over my clit and the fire breaks free and rages through me. I cry out, convulse below him as he strokes me and kisses me.

When I lay back, limp, but still burning for him, he lifts his head and smiles at me. My heart leaps at that smile and I grin back, like we just took on the world and won. Then he takes me in his arms and carries me to the long table. He lays me on it. I watch as he pulls off his shirt. His chest is muscular and slick with sweat. His shoulders are defined and strong. They'd have to be—he carries so much responsibility. It shows how much he cares.

My eyes catch the trail of dark hair leading down his abdomen to his pants. His fingers hesitate at his buttons. I look up into his eyes. He's giving me one last chance to change my mind.

"You promised," I say. "Heaven."

He doesn't wait for me to say more. He kicks off his pants and his length springs free. It's thick, hard and beautiful.

I sit up and pull my dress off and unsnap my bra. He looks thunderstruck.

"Come here," I say.

I don't have to say it twice. He climbs onto the table and pushes me back to the cool wood. The length of his body presses into mine, his skin on mine, touching everywhere. Heaven.

I never realized it, but it's what I've been waiting for my whole life.

"Jessie," he whispers, there's aching love in his voice.

Then he takes my wrists and shackles them in his hands. He presses them above my head and holds me down.

"I won't let you go," he says.

"Who says I'll let you?" I tilt my hips up to him in offering. He plunges inside me.

Who knew that heaven would feel so much like coming home?

15

WILL

I THRUST into Jessie and her tight heat surrounds me. White stars explode across my vision as she clamps around me and I shout out. I almost spend on the first thrust because of the ecstasy of feeling her around me.

She cries out and I grab her mouth with mine and catch her cries of pleasure. Nothing, nothing has ever felt so good. I hold myself still above her and take a moment to let the world realign. I never knew I could feel so much happiness, so much joy. I look into her eyes. They're bright and filled with the emotion I always dreamed of seeing and never believed I would. If there was ever any doubt, now there's none—she's the only woman I will ever love.

"I want you," she whispers.

I press my forehead to hers and hold her gaze. "I'll always want you," I say. "I'll always love you" is what I mean.

"I need you," she says.

I let go of her wrists and link my hands with hers. When I do, she pulses around me and I growl at the sensation. Slowly, I pull out of her, leaving her warmth. When I do, the world seems darker. She raises her hips to me and I thrust back in. She cries out and I kiss her, press into her, try to connect in as many places as possible.

I reach down between us and flick my fingers over her clit. As soon as I do, she pulses around me and I feel the pulse over my whole body. I stroke her clit and thrust in and out of her, driving into her warmth.

"Jessie."

She wraps her legs around me and grabs my lower back. She pulls me deeper.

"I'm not letting you go either," she says.

Her words release the last of my restraint. I grab her mouth and kiss her, let it tell her all the things I haven't yet said.

You're mine. You've always been mine. I love you. I'm sorry I didn't come to you earlier. I'm sorry I wasn't ready.

I love you.

I strum her clit, suck her tongue, taste her, let her taste my love. I bury myself in her as deep as I can go until I can't tell where I end and she begins. I can't separate her pleasure from mine. She's clenching around me, pulling the pleasure out of me, the world disappears, and it's just us. The two of us.

She cries out, holds me so tight that all thought leaves me— there's only feeling.

She grabs my back and holds me inside her. I ride her wave, sink into her pleasure and the joy in her eyes. The pressure inside me builds, I can't stop, I never want to stop.

She's mine. She's mine.

At that thought, pleasure explodes, she gives a final trembling clamp around me and I spill myself, all my love, inside her.

∾

"Do you know what I like best about you?" Jessie asks.

"What?" I quirk an eyebrow at her, then look back down and keep running my fingers over the curve of her bare thigh. I love how it's rounded and soft and dips to her hip bone and the line of her stomach. I place a kiss on the top of her hip bone and start to trail down her leg.

She lets out a gasp and I smile up at her.

"Let me guess. What you like best about me is my home library?"

We're in my bedroom back home. I brought her here after we cleaned up the library and grabbed dinner to-go from Tybalt's. We ate grilled scallops in bed, made love, had chocolate mousse, made love again. It's one in the morning, Jessie is naked in my bed, and I've never been happier.

She laughs and swats at my arm. "Nooo, not your home library. Although, it is impressive and strangely a massive turn-on."

I grin. When we got here I gave her a tour of my thousand-book library.

"Obviously," I say and wink at her. Then, "Is it my homes in New York and London? You're a city girl at heart?"

She scowls at me. "Be serious. I'm planning on living in Romeo the rest of my life. I'll raise my kids here, babysit my grandkids here. New York and London have nothing on Romeo."

At her words my mouth goes dry. I can see it so clearly. Jessie in the meadow with a baby in her arms, a toddler rolling in the grass next to her. She smiles and looks up at a man. Her soul mate. His back is to me. I can't see his face.

My chest tightens.

"You want kids?" I ask, my voice comes out rough.

She shifts on her elbow and puts her chin in her hand. Her eyes grow happy. "I want a house full of kids, so that the halls are always full of laughter and noise. The more noise the more love."

I reach out and run my hand down her cheek. "That sounds wonderful. And Romeo's just the place for it."

If I had my way, I'd make sure she spent the rest of her life surrounded by noise and laughter and love. I know how much living in a silent house hurt her.

"Could you live here year round?" she asks.

"So that's what you're aiming at. You like me best for my house. It'll easily fit, what...ten, twelve kids?"

She snorts, then starts laughing. "You nailed it. It's your *massive* house I'm attracted to." She wags her eyebrows suggestively.

I laugh and grab her, pull her under me. I kiss her nose, her cheeks, her lips.

"Tell me," I say.

She stills and shifts under me until she's comfortably nestled in my arms.

"Well, I guess it's not actually just one thing," she says.

I'm suddenly, strangely nervous about what she's going to say. She reaches over and places her hand over my heart. Her fingers drift over me, stroking gently.

"I've seen you at work, you're skilled, powerful, clearly the best at what you do. I used to purposely sit near you when you worked in the park or outside the bakery and listen to your phone calls. I was always amazed at how you handled crises or treated your employees with so much respect. Even when I didn't want to, I admired you."

I frown. "The thing you like best about me is my business acumen?"

She shifts. "No. I'm not done explaining. It's hard for me to put it in words." She presses her palm to my chest.

I smile. I do like the part where she admitted she sought me out. She's been as drawn to me as I have to her.

She continues, "I love that you keep coming to Romeo, and that you've never flaunted your wealth or status. You're humble and real. You work hard, you take care of your family. You're loyal. You're calm and steady, unless you want something badly, then you go after it with all your determination." She looks at me with a smile. "So I like that you're you. Everything that makes you you. I like that you like triple espressos in the mornings, and roast beef sandwiches. I like that you work the Europe and Asia hours so you can have the day to yourself. I like that you love books and climbing trees and kissing in the rain. I like that you love small towns and that you believe in the power of a hot cup of tea, a book, and a friend to share both with. I love all that about you."

My chest expands, filling with her words. I imagine us five years from now, in this bed, warm under a pillowy down comforter, the fire going, a pot of tea on the nightstand, and a pile of books nearby. She's in my arms in that dream.

"Is that all?" I ask, happiness in my voice. I place a kiss on her mouth.

"One more thing," she says.

I nod, and while she's thinking, I position myself over her, nudge open her legs and slide my length into her warmth.

"Yes?" I ask.

She makes a small noise in her throat and runs her hands over my shoulders.

"I like best that when I'm with you, I want to be with you, for the good, for the bad, for the always."

I think I like that best too.

I kiss her and take us to heaven.

16

JESSIE

I CRACK another egg into the bowl and start to whisk. It's seven in the morning, Will's still in bed. I woke up curled into his side, my head on his chest, his arms around me. I smile and start to hum while I whisk up the eggs for omelets.

We stayed up until almost four in the morning talking and making love. There's not a doubt in my mind—Will is my soul mate. Somehow I misunderstood Miss Erma. Will is mine.

I pour the eggs into the hot buttered skillet and add the ham and cheese while it cooks. I have to be at work by nine, but there's time for breakfast in bed. Hopefully he likes it. I slide the cooked omelet onto a plate, position it on a tray next to two cups of coffee, buttered toast, blackberry jam, a plate of crispy bacon, and two freshly squeezed orange juices.

"Breakfast? For me?" His voice teases from the entry to the kitchen.

I smile and a happy warmth flows over me. "I was going to bring it up," I say. I turn around with a grin.

It's not Will.

My cheeks heat and embarrassment fills me. "Gavin," I squeak. "Hi."

I smile and swallow the lump in my throat.

His eyes light with humor. He's in pajama pants and a t-shirt, and his hair is sticking up.

"I smelled bacon and coffee," he says. "I didn't know you were here, I thought you were Will."

I nod my head quickly, "Mhm."

I look down and catalog my appearance. When I got up, I threw on my white dress from yesterday. I'm barefoot, but I splashed water on my face and pulled my hair into a ponytail. Thank goodness I decided to get dressed in a proper outfit. I'd forgotten Gavin was here.

He quirks his eyebrows at me, sort of like Will but not, and smiles. It does nothing for me. Nothing at all. I smile with happiness. I love Will. I love him. I want nothing more than to go back upstairs and feed him breakfast and make love.

I beam at Gavin. This is wonderful. I don't love him, not at all, not one bit.

He looks at me, and a slightly stunned expression crosses his face. I pull back on the full magnitude smile.

"I'm so glad you came down," I say. Because it proved one hundred percent, without a doubt that he's not for me. "Have some bacon."

I shift the plate toward him. He can have all the bacon he likes if it means he'll go away and I can go upstairs to Will.

I'm going to wake Will up and tell him I love him. Happiness fills me until I feel like I'm going to burst.

"Sooo...I know why you're here," Gavin says.

He steps to the counter and leans against it. I look toward the entryway, eager to get upstairs.

"Yeah?" I ask, distracted by the memory of Will half-covered by the bed sheets.

"Because you're my soul mate."

His words knock me upside the head. I shake my head and try to rearrange what he just said, but it still sounds the same.

"What?"

His lip curls in a satisfied smile. "You're my soul mate."

"Nope." I hold up my hands and take a step back. "No, I'm not. Not your soul mate."

His eyes take on a look that I don't like. Sort of like the expression of someone about to jump out of a plane when they really don't want to but are determined to anyway.

"I'm really not," I say.

He nods. "You are. A little old lady from town visited me yesterday. She explained the whole thing. She showed me a book, told me that we're meant to be, that it's fate."

I can't get a breath. Miss Erma came here? Told Gavin that he and I are..."No."

He takes a step toward me. My heart thuds.

"She said lots of people fight it, but you can't deny what's meant to be."

Holy crap. My once-upon-a-time fantasy is actually my worst nightmare. Gavin holds out his hand to me. I grab a slice of crispy bacon and hold it up like a sword. He looks at the bacon and lets out a short laugh.

"That's awesome. En garde." He plucks the bacon from my hand and takes a bite.

I back away. "There's a misunderstanding. I'm not your soul mate."

"This is really good." He grabs another slice of bacon and takes a bite. "Heck. I'll love you just for your bacon."

I sputter. "You don't love me and I don't love you. At all."

He nods and takes a sip of the orange juice.

"Hey! That's not yours," I cry in indignation.

"Course it is. You came here to make me breakfast because

you can't resist fate. Just like you always stared at me when we were kids-"

"I didn't!"

"Did. It's because we're soul mates. Same reason you invited me to dinner and out biking. Because I'm like the flame to your moth. The love of your life."

I shake my head in denial. "You have a fiancée. You're getting married."

He scowls and I think I've put some sense into him, but then he shakes his head.

"I was bound to screw that up. It's what I do. And clearly it's because you're the one for me. You can't screw up with a soul mate."

I let out a frustrated sigh. "You're delusional."

He grins at me. "We'll go to South Africa on safari, see the sunrise on Mount Fuji, dive the Great Barrier Reef—"

"I don't dive. I don't climb. I don't safari. I'm not doing those things with you. I have a few weeks of vacation a year and I'm spending those here, in Romeo."

He wrinkles his forehead. "That's weird."

I throw up my hands. "We have nothing in common."

"Opposites attract," he says and nods sagely.

Oh my gosh. Is this what I was like? So blind?

"Look, Gavin."

"Yes?" He smiles and steps closer.

"We're not soul mates," I say slowly.

"Call her."

"What?"

"Call the lady, see what she says."

I shake my head. "No. Because it doesn't matter to me."

He gives me a skeptical look and I sigh.

"It's because you know it's true. We're meant to be," he says.

A week ago I would've rejoiced at those words. Now I just want him to take them back.

Then, Gavin gets that funny look on his face, like he's leaping out of that plane. He steps toward me, tips my chin up and swoops down.

In a millisecond I register that he's kissing me. And his is the wrong mouth, the wrong feel, the wrong everything. It's...gross.

I move to shove him away but he steps back.

"That was—" he starts. His mouth turns down. Obviously he didn't like it either. Idiot.

I let out a long breath and put my hand on his arm, ready to tell him it's his brother who's mine. "Look, Gavin—"

"The wedding is off, you monumental prick!"

I jerk my hand off his arm and swing toward the kitchen entry.

"Lacey. You're early," Gavin says. He sounds dumbstruck.

But I barely hear him. Because standing in the entry next to Lacey, and an older couple, her parents, I think, is Will.

The look on Will's face—my heart starts to gallop at that look.

His eyes are full of self-mockery and understanding of what he thinks I've done. His jaw clenches, his lips flatten, and his eyes that were so full of warmth last night leach back to cold.

"We didn't, it's not...it's not what it looks like," I say, and then I almost let out a hysterical giggle at how cliché, how stupid that sounded.

"As you were lip-locked in an embrace," says Lacey's father, "I'd say it's exactly what it looked like." He turns to Will. "The merger's off. You'll hear from my lawyers."

"Lacey," Gavin says. He starts toward her.

She holds up her hand. "Don't." Her face drains of color.

She's in a gray sheath dress and trench coat. She looks smart and stylish and completely heartbroken.

Gavin stops in front of her. "Let me explain."

A tear trails down her cheek and she angrily wipes it away. She looks from Gavin to me and back at Gavin. I feel ill with shame. I may not have wanted this to happen this morning, but until yesterday I was actively trying to make it happen. I look at the hurt, confusion and pain in Lacey's face and I realize that I was selfish and pigheaded and plain wrong in my pursuit of Gavin. Of a soul mate. I was wrong. My actions hurt other people.

"I love...loved you," Lacey says. "I was going to marry you."

"Please. You don't understand—" I say.

"She's my soul mate," Gavin interrupts.

The words fall like a bomb into the room. I'm stunned into silence. Lacey lets out a strangled laugh. Then she marches over to the counter and picks up the two glasses of orange juice. She flings one in Gavin's face. He flinches as the juice hits him. Then she dumps the other juice over my head. I gasp as the cold liquid runs through my hair and onto my face.

Lacey sets down the glasses on the counter and wipes her hands.

"I don't want to hear from you ever again. I'm worth more than a man-child who doesn't honor his word." Lacey swipes another tear, then turns away, her head high, and walks out of the kitchen.

Her mom, a small woman who looks just like her but with fine wrinkles and glasses, rushes after her. Mr. Duporte, a big-fisted, ex-football-player-turned-businessman type, puffs his chest out.

"As my daughter said, we'll communicate through the lawyers."

Will gives Mr. Duporte a cordial nod. He looks distant and

cold. Since I spoke, he hasn't once looked at me.

"I'll give you a ride back to your bed and breakfast," Will says.

"Like hell." Mr. Duporte swings toward him and levels Will with a glare.

Will quirks an eyebrow. "Your taxi's gone. It will be another thirty minutes minimum for it to return. Your choice."

Mr. Duporte scowls. "I'll meet you outside."

Will turns to follow him, not even giving Gavin or me a glance. As if, for him, I've ceased to exist. Desperation fills me. I thought he'd promised he wouldn't let me go. That if I chose Gavin he'd steal me and lock me away so I'd always be his. What about that promise?

"Will," I say.

His back is turned but he pauses at the kitchen entry.

"Please. Look at me."

He turns around slowly. I wipe the orange juice off my face. When he finally focuses on me I give him a hesitant smile.

His bottom lip quivers, but then he presses his mouth flat. His eyes flicker to a warmer blue at my smile but then they snap to cold and impersonal. My heart cracks. It's like before, when I'd smile and he'd look away. Except it's not exactly the same as before, because now I love him and I think he loves me. I'm not choosing Gavin over him, not ever. I'm not choosing some fantasy of a soul mate. I don't want a fantasy. I want him.

"Will," says Gavin. "Sorry about the merger. I didn't want that to happen."

Will looks at Gavin and gives a curt nod but doesn't say anything.

"We're soul mates, Jessie and me, can you believe it?" There's a hollow note in Gavin's voice.

Will turns to look at me and lifts an eyebrow sardonically. "No, I can't. You must be so happy."

"We're not soul mates," I say to Gavin. I turn to Will. "We're not."

"Call her," Gavin says.

"What? Call who?"

"The old lady. Call her. Confirm it. I need to know I didn't lose my fiancée for nothing." There's a desperate light in Gavin's eyes, as if now that he's jumped from the plane, he realizes he doesn't have a parachute.

"Okay," I say. Then I flush. "I don't have my phone."

Will reaches into his pocket and holds his out to me. There's a bitter twist to his lips. I take it from his hand. He's careful not to touch me.

Erma picks up on the second ring. I don't waste time.

"Hi. Miss Erma, it's Jessie. Yesterday when you came by the Williams' house did you tell Gavin he was my soul mate?"

"Hmm? I didn't go by the Williams' house. I'm on a trip to NYC, I'm seeing the Rockettes with Wanda." I hear car horns honking from her end of the line. She's in New York City?

"What did the lady look like?" I ask Gavin.

He frowns. "Well, there were two of them. Looked like sisters, about eighty, one liked to joke, the other didn't."

Ohhh. It was Petunia and Gladiola. The meddling old birds. I knew this was a misunderstanding. Erma can clear it up and confirm that Will is mine. And then, Gavin can go and try to fix this mess with Lacey. And I can go hold Will.

"Miss Erma?"

"Yes?"

"Can you please tell me *exactly* what you saw when you had the vision of my soul mate?"

Will folds his arms over his chest and looks out the window. The sun streaks through the glass and falls across his shoulders. I want to reach out and hold him. Go back to last night and the warmth of his arms.

"Of course I can. I saw you as a little girl, you were sitting in an oak tree."

"Yes," I say, and my breath hitches.

Will turns back and watches my expression. His face is neutral, but I can feel all his attention laser focused on me and my reaction to what Erma says. Across the kitchen, Gavin watches tensely. He has no idea that this means more to Will than a failed business merger.

"And in the tree with you is a little boy. He gives you a hanky and you give him a flower. That boy is your soul mate."

My stomach plummets. Will's eyes are locked on mine and he sees her answer in my expression.

"Thank you," I whisper. I disconnect the call. My throat is tight and aching.

Will nods, and in his nod I see a finality. He's cutting off what we had. He's cutting the connection between us.

"Well?" Gavin asks.

I lick my dry lips, unable to look away from Will.

"What did she say?" Gavin says.

I swallow, unable to answer. I search Will's eyes for the man I know is there, but I don't see him. I see the stranger I thought he was.

Will can read my expression, he knows what Erma said. Before he said he didn't care, but now, for some reason, he does. He turns and walks out of the kitchen.

"What?" asks Gavin.

"You're not mine," I say, then I run after Will.

My bare feet slap against the cold hardwood as I rush after Will. He's fast. He's almost to the front door in the wide, formal receiving room. He's dressed in a tight t-shirt, jeans and leather shoes. His hair is sleep mussed and there's a love bite on his neck.

My love bite.

"Will. Wait."

He doesn't turn. I grab his arm when he reaches for the brass door handle. I pull him around.

"It doesn't matter what Erma says. I told you that it doesn't matter to me," I say.

He looks me over, and I'm suddenly uncomfortably aware that I'm in a wrinkled dress, covered in orange juice.

"You claim that, but the first chance you got you kissed my brother and confirmed with him and Erma that he's your 'soul mate,'" he says in that precise, clipped and distant voice.

"He's not! I didn't."

He raises an eyebrow.

"I mean yes, I did. He kissed me, I didn't kiss him. He misunderstood and thought that just because Erma said he and I are soul mates that I'd want him. I don't. I want you."

Hesitantly, I reach out and put my hand on his chest. It's as hard and unmoving as stone.

I look up at him and as scared as I am, I reach out. "I love you," I whisper.

I feel his chest shake beneath my hand. Then he steps back, out of my reach.

"It was a game," he says in a cold voice.

What? I stare at him. Shake my head in denial.

"You were right. I'd do anything to save the merger and keep you from ruining my brother's life."

I shake my head. "No."

He nods. "It was a game. Looks like I lost." He gives me a cold smile.

"No," I say again, my lips are numb.

He doesn't respond. Instead, he turns and walks away, shuts the door.

I stare at the door in shock. Then I sink to the floor, wrap my hands around my knees and cry.

17

WILL

It's a tense car ride to the Duportes' bed and breakfast. No one speaks, not even when I drop them off and they climb out of the car. I park in the lot. I have no idea what to do or where to go.

I lost her.

My mind keeps replaying the loop of Jessie and Gavin kissing, then Jessie on the phone, her expression removing all doubt.

I lost her.

I lost her. I lost her.

When I let the Duportes in and led them toward the savory breakfast smells and the quiet voices in the kitchen, I was thinking about leaving the entertaining of the Duportes to Gavin. I wanted to grab Jessie, pull her back upstairs and spend a full day in bed.

Gavin has never cooked a day in his life, so when I woke up and smelled toast and bacon and coffee, I knew it was Jessie cooking for us. I grinned at the ceiling like a lunatic. I felt like the luckiest man in the world. I have millions of dollars, offices around the globe, exotic homes, and none of it ever made me feel one tenth the joy of that moment.

I jumped out of bed, threw on clothes and hurried downstairs. When I saw the Duportes pull up I was disappointed, but then I heard Gavin's voice with Jessie in the kitchen and I knew I could leave them with him and haul Jessie away.

Until we walked in and I saw the kiss.

The world stopped. At first, I didn't understand. I saw them, their lips touching, but it didn't make any sense. My mind completely rejected it as a possibility. Then I heard Lacey gasp and my mind jerked, restarted and caught up with reality.

Which was, first, Jessie and Gavin were kissing less than three hours after Jessie and I had made love. Second, Jessie confirmed without a doubt that she and Gavin are soul mates.

"I lost her," I say out loud.

I look out over downtown. The bed and breakfast is on a hill and has a panoramic view of Main Street, the river, and the forested mountain in the distance. It's nearly eight in the morning and downtown Romeo is waking up. The lights are on in the dance studio and the Kwans are unlocking the front door of the hardware store. I see the Harts setting up a new chocolate display in their front window, and Mrs. Charles is pushing a cart of books onto the sidewalk. I stare at the books and think of Jessie spread out beneath me, a pile of books surrounding us.

I love you, she'd said. I close my eyes. I love you.

My hands clasp the steering wheel. The endless loop of her kissing Gavin and phoning Erma is interrupted by the memory of her words. I love you.

My mind starts to settle and I unclasp my hands from the steering wheel. I told Jessie it was all a game. My mouth tastes of shame at the memory. When I said it, I felt like I'd boarded a speeding train and I couldn't stop it or derail it. Everything I'd always feared had happened. I'd given myself to Jessie, wanted her more than anything in the world. When I was young, my father would take people away. This time, when I risked more than I ever have before, fate took Jessie away.

It felt the same, but more cruel. And when it happened, my emotions shut down and I went backwards more than a decade. I was that boy again—the fifteen-year-old in the tree, telling the girl I loved that I didn't want her and didn't need her.

That it was a game.

My shoulders tense. I'm seeing a vision of the next thirty years. That image of Jessie in the field with her children? In it, her soul mate's back was turned—is that because I knew all along she'd choose Gavin?

No.

I take a deep breath. I'm not a kid anymore. I'm not beholden to old patterns and old emotions.

I'm going to go back, tell Jessie I'm sorry and that I love her. Then I'm keeping my promise and carrying her off to be mine.

The only person who is stopping me from being with her, is me.

I pull out of the lot and make it back to the house. It's a few minutes past eight. I rush into the house and pause to listen. I hear voices coming from the living room. I hurry toward them.

Gavin is talking with Jessie. He may be my brother and my best friend, but he's going to have to step aside or we're going to have problems.

I walk through the arched entry to the living room and come to a sudden stop. Jessie and Gavin are on the couch. Jessie's face is turned to Gavin's and she's speaking passionately. Gavin is completely absorbed in what she's saying. He reaches out and squeezes her hands, then her face lights up and she throws her arms around him. He holds her.

The breath whooshes out of me. The hollow place in my chest that I thought had been filled expands and starts to swallow me. I feel the coldness come over me—the protective layer I used to keep away the pain of losing the people I love.

I slowly take a quiet step backward, then another, until I'm back in my car and heading south toward NYC.

When I saw Jessie hug Gavin, another thought came to me. That book. The one Jessie showed me with hundreds of soul mates. All of them were happy, married, in love and together for their whole lives.

If I took Jessie and married her, would she regret it two years, ten years, twenty years from now? She may not love Gavin today, but she could in the future. And the love she said she feels for me, it could turn into a cage of resentment and disillusionment.

There's a saying which I always thought was trite and stupid —if you love someone let them go.

It's not trite, it's the hardest thing I've ever done.

I've loved Jessie from the first moment I saw her. For twenty years I've been holding onto her. It's time I let her go.

I want her to be happy. I want Gavin to be happy. Now, I suppose I'm glad I told Jessie it was all a game. It lets her be free to have a future without any guilt or regret or what ifs. She can think of me as a malicious bastard and I can stay far away.

I make it to my Manhattan office by lunch. Justin Van Cleeve, the extremely expensive lawyer that I keep on retainer, meets me at the elevator door. He's usually immaculately dressed in a business suit and tie, but today his suit is wrinkled and his tie is undone. He has bags under his eyes.

"I've been calling and texting since last night," Justin says.

"You've got DEFCON 1 here. Were you in the hospital? Dead? Abducted by aliens? Will, you've got problems."

I shove aside the pain of Jessie and Gavin and focus on Justin. A business crisis. Since last night? Not the merger then.

Perfect.

I can handle business. It doesn't require emotions, or friendship, or feelings.

"What is it? Get me up to speed."

We walk into my office. Justin closes the glass door and lowers the blinds. "Your assistant booked your jet to London. He has your suitcase and passport ready. The helicopter lands on the roof to take you to the airport in"—he looks at his watch —"twenty minutes."

I raise an eyebrow. "Any reason I'm flying to London today?" Not that I'm unhappy about the distraction.

Justin rubs his eyes. He looks like he had a terrible night. "There's an army of lawyers camped out in your London office. With your father. He's claiming legal ownership of the entire company. It's garbage, but they've got thousands of pages of documents and enough legal weaselry to stall your company's progress and earnings for years. It's takeover attempt number three. Your father said, and I quote, 'I'm not leaving this office until Will meets me face to face like a man instead of hiding behind his two-bit lawyer like a frightened child.' Frankly, I take offense at the two-bit jab."

Justin finishes his pronouncement and waits for my response.

I do the only thing I can. I laugh, and when I see the shocked expression on Justin's face I laugh even harder.

"It *was* aliens," he says. "They abducted you, didn't they?"

Which makes me laugh even more. Justin stares in shock. And suddenly I realize that in the five years he's worked with me he's never seen me laugh. He's constantly making jokes, but I doubt I ever even cracked a smile.

I'd kept myself locked away and everyone at a distance.

I stop chuckling and wipe my eyes. I'm looking forward to this meeting with my father. It's time I moved past the past.

"Did the Duporte lawyers contact you about the merger falling apart?"

"What?" Justin asks. He drops his face into his hands and moans. "Will, what have you been doing?"

Guess not.

"You realize this means you get to rack up billable hours, right? You should be breaking out the champagne at your windfall. A takeover attempt and a merger failure all in one day. Happy times for lawyer-kind."

Justin lifts his head. "Who are you and where is the real Will Williams? The real Will is a scary efficient, robotic genius who doesn't understand humor. What have you done with him?"

I smile, but it's covering a sharp pain. I wonder if I'll ever be able to go back to how I was, or if opening up to Jessie changed me forever. "I'll see you tomorrow," I say, ignoring Justin's comment.

It shouldn't take too long to get rid of an army of lawyers. While I'm at it I can forget about Jessie. Or at least practice not thinking about her every minute of every day.

It's early morning when I arrive at the London office. The city is covered in a wet, gray, misty rain. The streets are full of puddles and water run-off and everyone but me has an umbrella. Which means that when I step into the conference room, I'm damp and chilled.

I look around the space. Justin was wrong, it's not an army of lawyers, merely fifteen to twenty. I'm certain that only one of them has been practicing long enough to be a senior partner. I focus on him.

"Leave us," I say.

The older lawyer glances at my father.

My father, who I'd avoided looking at, nods. The lawyer gestures to his team of colleagues and they file out of the conference room.

I stand stone still, my hands folded behind my back, as they file past me. The last one out closes the door. Finally, I shift my gaze to my father. I haven't seen him since his last takeover attempt before my twenty-first birthday. His hair is thinning at the edges and turning silver. I remember with some surprise that he turned sixty this year. He's not as large as I remember and his presence doesn't have the same effect on me anymore.

"Well, I'm here," I say. "What now? The usual? You make threats with your lawyers. I make threats back. I win, you go back to Dubai and your mistress for another few years?"

My father doesn't seem to hear. He's taking in my appearance, cataloging all the details, like a man who thought he'd seen his last sunrise but is finally seeing another.

I stand awkwardly, hands clasped behind my back, and wait for him to respond. Finally he sighs and nods at the table.

"Tea?" he asks in a gruff voice.

There's a tea service on the long conference table. Buttery scones, chocolate biscuits, jam and clotted cream, a large teapot and mugs. My throat tightens as I think about tea and Jessie. I wonder what my twelve-year-old self would've told her about this meeting.

I shove the thought aside.

"No," I say. "Let's get down to business. This will be your last takeover attempt. The next time you try, I will ruin you. I'm done playing." I sit in a leather chair and lean back.

My father takes a seat diagonal to me and pours himself a cup of tea. Steam puffs up and is followed by the scent of bergamot and black tea leaves.

I close my eyes. Does everything have to evoke her?

"How's your brother?"

Something's different. I look at my father. Really look. "Gavin's fine." Then, "What's happened?"

He gives me a sheepish smile. "I'm a dad again. You have a brother."

I'm stunned. He's...what?

"Delia and I got married. She wants a big family." He holds out his hands and gives another sheepish smile.

My eyebrows lower. I have another brother? My heart starts to thump and I realize I already love him, within ten seconds of learning he exists, I love my baby brother.

My breath catches. I wonder what leverage my father will use, what upper hand he'll try to gain if he sees I care. I want to ask a thousand questions. What's his name, how old is he, what's he like, what color are his eyes, does he smile?

I school my features into an expressionless mask. But still, I care about this baby boy that I may never meet.

I lean forward, surprised at the vehemence I feel, and address my father. "If I hear even a whisper of a rumor that you treat your son the way you treated Gavin and me, I will destroy you. I will take you apart piece by piece and leave you ruined."

My father takes a drink of tea, not perturbed in the least. He sets down the cup, then, "Good. I'll hold you to that."

"Excuse me?"

He frowns and drags his hand over his chin. "I've spent a good majority of the past seven years thinking about my life and regretting most of it. There's a lot I did that I'll never forgive myself for. Especially how I treated you boys. I'll never forgive myself for that."

I swallow a lump in my throat. His words sound eerily similar to ones I said only a few days ago.

He continues, "Delia has helped me look forward. She's certain I can learn from my mistakes, acknowledge what I did, and not do it again. Move forward."

"Yet here we are," I say. "Another takeover attempt."

My father shifts uncomfortably. "Funny enough, the only way in the past ten years I've been able to see you is when I'm trying to take over your company." He shrugs. "I wanted to speak with you."

I stare at him. "You hired two dozen lawyers so we could have a chat over tea?"

He clears his throat. "Three dozen," then, "Delia said it was a bad idea."

I spread my hands. "Obviously."

My father nods. "I don't have the right to ask for a relationship. I don't expect one. I put all my fears and self-loathing on you boys, and for that I'm sorry. It took me nearly sixty years to grow up."

I study him. He's in an understated suit, unlike his former flashy Armani suits. He wears a simple gold wedding band and I allow myself to see that he seems relaxed, content with himself, centered.

"About destroying me and tearing me apart for my son..."

"Yes?"

"I'd like to invite you to his christening. His name's Tyler." He pulls out his wallet and flips it open to a small photo of a tiny baby in a blue hat and a diaper. A dark-haired woman smiles down at him. My chest hurts looking at the picture.

"Is that Delia?"

"That's her. We're married now. Two years in November."

I nod. I didn't even know my dad had remarried.

"When's the christening?"

My dad smiles and it's filled with enormous relief and gratitude.

"I'm not doing it for you," I say. "I'm doing it for my brother. Every kid deserves as much unconditional love from as many people as possible."

My dad sniffs and blinks his eyes. "Good. Good," he says in a gruff voice. He holds out his hand to shake. I grasp it in a firm grip. I don't think I've ever shaken his hand before.

"I never told you," he says. "but I've always been proud of you. Tremendously proud."

I frown. "Because I became the focused businessman you wanted?"

He shakes his head. "Because no matter how hard I tried to ruin it, you kept your ability to care."

I stare down at the table, unable to look at him. It was Jessie that did that for me. If I hadn't met her, if I hadn't fallen in love at first sight, if she hadn't given me *The Horse and His Boy*, and all her years of smiles, I would've lost the ability to care long ago.

I stand up abruptly and shove back the chair. "I have to go."

My father looks stunned. I hand him my card with my private cell number. "Send the details. I'll be there."

"Will you tell Gavin? I don't have any way of contacting him. He doesn't have a company to mock-take over for catch-up chats. I'd like to ask him to come."

"I'll tell him."

My dad nods then offers his hand again. I take it and give him a firm clasp.

"Thank you," I say.

"For what?"

"For reminding me of something I'd forgotten."

166

I leave him standing in the conference room and rush down to the busy streets of London. There's a passage I underlined in Jessie's copy of *The Horse and His Boy*. In it Aslan tells Shasta that no one is told any story but their own. I don't know Jessie's story. I don't know if it's true whether or not Gavin is her soul mate. Her story isn't mine, although our stories intersect. But I know my story, and in it I've loved Jessie all my life, with all my heart. Right now, I don't know the ending, but I do know the next chapter.

18

JESSIE

IT'S FUNNY, when I finally got everything I thought I ever wanted it turned out that I was wanting the wrong thing. I slide the pile of romance books and romcoms into the library book drop. They fall and hit the bottom with a dull thud. All the formulas and the meet-cutes and the ways people fall in love in fiction—none of it is real.

I spent my entire life hiding behind fantasies and books.

I shove the books into the slot and let them go—I used them for the formulas, but love doesn't have rules. You can't make someone love you and you can't choose who you love.

Before she died, my mom told me that in a town like Romeo you're guaranteed to find your true love. It's not a matter of if, but when.

The back of my eyes sting and my throat tightens.

"What's wrong, dear?"

I look over. It's Wanda. She's early for the seniors' computer class. Gladiola and Petunia stand behind her near the circulation desk.

I press my lips together and sniff. I shove the last of the

books into the drop and try to swipe at my eyes without them seeing.

Wanda sets her hand on my arm. "Dear? What is it?"

I drop my head. "I think," I whisper, "that if my mom were alive, she'd be ashamed of me."

I look at the carpet and my throat burns with the tears I don't want to let out.

"Dear, no," cries Wanda.

She glances around the library at all the patrons and then back to me. Then she takes my arm and pulls me into the community room. Gladiola and Petunia follow her in and shut the door.

"Tell me," Wanda says in a stern grandma voice.

Petunia starts to say something but Wanda shushes her.

I close my eyes and blink back the tears. "I've always wanted my mom to be proud of me." My voice shakes at my admission. "I imagine her looking down and watching over me, and everything I've done, I've always wanted her to be proud, to be glad I'm hers. Even though she's not here with me, I've always believed she can see me and that she's proud."

I swipe at my eyes.

"She is," Wanda says. "We all know she is. Your mom loved you, she would be so proud of who you've become."

I shake my head no and look away. They don't know how many people I've hurt with my stubbornness and selfishness.

"My mom used to tell me the story, of how in Romeo, you always find your true love. The day of her funeral, I thought she sent me mine and that Gavin was her message to me that she was still with me and that love still survived. And hope. And kindness. And...that even though she was gone, I could still be loved."

"Oh, sweetheart." Wanda pulls me into her arms and sets my head to her shoulder. I breathe in the familiar scent of her lily of the valley perfume. "She loves you. She's proud. We all are."

"We are," Gladiola says.

"That's right. Everyone in Romeo is proud. And we love you too," Petunia says.

I pull away and sniff. "My mom told me that story so I'd be open to finding love. But I did it wrong. I hurt people."

I think of Lacey, her stricken expression. Gavin caught up in it all, and Will. I saw the moment his heart broke. The light in his eyes flickered and died. He pulled himself back into that cold, lonely, distant place where he doesn't let anyone close.

"What happened?" Petunia asks.

So I tell them. I tell them how I've been chasing the wrong Romeo. How my blind belief that Gavin was the one, and my disregard for other people resulted in losing the man I loved. I tell them how Erma predicted Gavin as my soul mate but that it doesn't matter, because I need to stop trusting stories and fantasies and predictions and start trusting myself. And my heart knows that Will has always been the one.

"Will's been gone for two days," I say. "And I don't know that he'll ever come back."

Everyone is quiet. Then Petunia and Gladiola give each other a speaking glance.

"I told you your old lady busybody routine would catch up and bite you, Petunia," says Gladiola.

"Bite me? You're the one who said we needed to help things along like a fairy godmother. Fairy godmother, my tush. Look at Jessie, she's devastated."

"Hush," Wanda says, and she pats my arm.

"Bah. Rotten pumpkin, fairy godmother nonsense," mutters Gladiola.

I smile even though my heart's not into it. Wanda, eyes

bright behind her horn-rimmed glasses, notices the wobble in my smile.

"Well, dear, no matter what happens, rest assured, we are all proud of the woman you've become. It takes a lot of courage to admit you've been wrong. I'm sure your mom told you that."

I nod. She did.

"So what will you do?" Petunia asks.

I think about what I've done, who I've been and who I strive to be. I always wanted my mom to be proud, but now I realize I want to be proud of myself too.

"I'm going to tell the people I hurt that I'm sorry. And if Will won't come here, then I'll go to him."

The ladies cheer. We look up as the door to the computer room opens and Mr. Frank walks in.

"What'd I miss?" he asks.

"Class is canceled," I say. "I'm going to go find my true love."

"WE'RE LANDING IN FIVE MINUTES," GAVIN SAYS. HE LOOKS OVER at me from the pilot's seat. "Nervous?"

"No," I say. It turns out, in addition to all his other extreme sports and stunts, Gavin also has his pilot's license and a small plane at Romeo's private airport. And he'd heard from Will two days ago that he was heading to NYC for a while.

"Did I mention how much more I'm going to like having you as a sister-in-law than a soul mate?" he asks. He was all too happy to fly me to the city and deliver me to his brother.

"Only about five hundred times."

"Good. Because as soon as we land, I'm going to win back my fiancée. I was a self-sabotaging idiot."

"Good luck," I say, and I wholeheartedly mean it.

He grins and his eyes crinkle.

"Do you think he'll show?" I ask.

"He'll show," Gavin says with utter confidence. "I know my brother, there's no way he won't show."

The lights of the New York area loom closer. We stop talking as Gavin takes the plane in for landing.

THE 102ND FLOOR OF THE EMPIRE STATE BUILDING IS COLD. THE air conditioning is on high and the sky is dark. The lights of the city surround me. The observatory is crowded, even though it's nearly ten at night. A family with six kids pushes past me to see the view. A middle-aged couple at the window kisses.

I clutch the red rose I bought at the vendor on the street and search the faces of the crowd.

He's not coming.

No matter Gavin's confidence in him or how much I wish it were different, Will isn't coming.

I left a message on his phone, telling him I had one last idiotic, ill-advised, romantic foolery left to win my true love. I promised him that he was going to hate it and he'd have to try to stop me—because that's what friends did.

I told him I'd be waiting at the top of the Empire State Building, holding a red rose...and my heart. Both of them were for him.

Please come, I'd said. *I'll be there at ten o'clock. Please come.*

I walk closer to the window and peer down at the street below. I half expect to see him jump out of a taxi. But I don't.

He's not here. He's not coming.

"Ma'am. The elevators are leaving." The guard motions at the elevator and I take one last look at the panoramic view of the city and the emptying observatory.

At the street level exit I throw the rose into the garbage. I think about how Will threw away *The Horse and His Boy* all those years ago.

But he went back for it. He went back.

I'll wait. Maybe he's racing toward me, scared he'll be too late. I lean my back against the side of the building and scan the street.

An hour passes. Then another. Midnight comes and goes. I start to get nervous as the street grows more deserted. He's not coming.

I open my purse and pull out the tattered old copy of our book. I flip through the pages. Near the end, I catch a paragraph underlined in dark ink.

My eyes fill with tears. It's the paragraph where Cor and Aravis decide to marry, because they were so used to fighting and making up that they got married so they could do it more easily. Next to it in a boyish scrawl is the word *us*, and a date from nearly fifteen years ago. I flip through the pages again and find one last underline. It's one of my favorites too. It always made me feel better whenever I read it.

It says that when your life goes wrong, it usually keeps getting worse and worse until things turn around, and when they do, it all keeps getting better and better and beautifully better.

I wipe my eyes, close the book, and put it back in my purse.

I never knew how beautifully better life could be until I opened up to Will.

I search the streets again.

He's not coming.

I walk toward Grand Central Station. I'll catch the late train north, toward home. My grand romantic plan failed. I smile ruefully. They always do, don't they?

∿

THE BARK OF THE OLD OAK TREE SCRATCHES MY LEGS. I LEAN BACK into the trunk and lift the binoculars to my eyes. The house is still empty. Will's not here. I got back to Romeo early this morning, in time for a quick nap, and then work.

I drop the binoculars and lean my head back against the tree. The sun is setting, and the warm air, the singing bugs, and the soft swaying of the branches lulls me.

Will didn't come. He hasn't answered his phone or responded to any texts. I let out a long sigh. I should've gone back to bed, but something in me needed to come to the old oak.

A twig snaps below me. My eyes fly open. I look down and my heart starts to gallop.

It's Will. He looks up at me, eyes inscrutable.

"What are you doing in my tree?" he asks.

My eyebrows crease, then I lift my binoculars. "Being a peeping Tom," I say. A sliver of hope works its way into my heart.

His lips start to curve then stop. He grabs the lowest limb and hoists himself up. He climbs up the tree and spans the fifteen feet in seconds. When he reaches me he sits down next to me on the branch.

"Hello, William."

"Jessie."

When he says my name it feels like he's touched me everywhere—my whole body heats.

He looks forward toward the sunset, not at me. I turn to it too and let my speeding heart slow to a steady rhythm. The sky is dusky blue and painted with bright orange and golden clouds.

"Why were you crying?" he finally asks in a low, quiet voice.

I startle and realize there must be tear tracks on my cheeks. I look over at him. His face is covered in a few days' worth of dark stubble, he has bags under his eyes and his clothes are dirty and wrinkled. To me, he's the most beautiful man in the world.

"Because I lost my best friend. The person I love most in the whole world." My voice is thick with emotion.

He nods solemnly, scoots closer and puts his arm around my shoulder.

"I'm sorry," he says. "I lost the person I love, too. I thought it was because she didn't love me."

"But she does."

He nods. "She does."

I let out a sharp exhale. "What happened? Where did you go?"

"London. I got you this." He shifts and pulls a book from his pocket. "It's signed. I got you first editions of the entire series, all signed."

The sliver of hope in my heart grows and I smile at him hesitantly. Smile back, I urge him silently.

"Why?" I ask, gesturing to the book.

He raises an eyebrow. "I thought if I promised to shower you with priceless rare books you might forgive me and reconsider heaven."

The look on his face is open and vulnerable. His arm tightens around my shoulder. He's terrified of my answer.

"Does heaven come with you?"

He closes his eyes. "Yes. That's the deal."

He still thinks I'm going to reject him. "Did you get my messages about New York?"

He looks at me, eyebrows drawn. "I lost my phone in London. I flew back as soon as I could. Then I came straight here. I looked for you everywhere, I..." He stops when he sees the look on my face. "What is it?"

"I waited for you at the top of the Empire State Building."

A stunned look crosses his face. "You did what?"

I smile. "I thought I'd recreate a final romance cliché just for you."

"That's a terrible idea," he says. His lips quirk in an almost smile and his eyes turn a lighter shade of blue.

"I knew you'd see it that way." My smile grows.

"I love you," he says. And the way he says it is like a prayer. I clasp his hand and lean my head to his chest. I press my lips to his beating heart.

"I love you," I whisper. Then, "You're not letting me go?"

"Never," he swears. "I'm sorry I left. I'm sorry I didn't listen."

"I don't want Gavin."

"I know."

"Can I tell you a story?" I ask.

"Always." He pulls me tighter against his side and we look toward the glowing sunset.

"Once upon a time," I begin, "there was a little girl who wanted very badly to love and be loved. And when she met a little boy in this very tree, she thought he was *the one*. She idolized him and dreamed about him. But there was another boy who she didn't idolize, who she claimed she didn't even like. He was like a thorn in the bottom of her foot. Every time she drifted too far into the fantasy of the other boy, he'd poke her and pull her back to focus on him. Until finally, the girl realized she'd been wrong all along. That she didn't love the boy from Erma's vision, she loved the thorn, the man that kept waking her up from her dream—to live her real life, her best life, with him."

Will reaches over and takes my hand. "Good story. Out of curiosity, what was Erma's vision?"

I shrug. "The day my mom died, she saw that I met a boy. We climbed up this tree. He gave me his handkerchief and I gave him a flower. She said he was my soul mate."

Will stiffens and slowly takes his arm from my shoulders and pulls his hand out of mine.

"It's not real," I say. My mouth goes dry.

Will slowly shakes his head. "Unbelievable."

"She's wrong. We both know, this time Miss Erma's wrong." He needs to believe this.

What's the matter with him?

"Come with me," he says, and there's an odd note in his voice.

He drops down to the ground and I scramble after him. When I get to the grass he grabs my hand.

"What? What is it?"

He shakes his head. "Come on." He pulls me across the field, first at a fast walk, then at a run.

"Will, what?" I gasp.

We're heading toward the house, the tall meadow grass bends around us and white night moths fly up into the air as we pass.

"I'm not going with Gavin, I told you. I don't want him."

If he's taking me to the house to find his brother, I'll bonk him over the head with a hardback encyclopedia.

We reach the front door. I'm out of breath. Will's breathing hard and there's a strange light in his eyes. The same light he had when we first made love, and when he promised he'd never let me go.

He unlocks the door and pulls me up the stairs. We stop in his bedroom suite.

"You loved that little boy?" he asks, his voice rough.

I shake my head no. "I love you," I say.

He nods and gently pushes me back to the bed. I sit down on the thick comforter.

"You loved him for years?" he asks.

"I thought I loved him. But I don't. I love you," I say firmly. I hold open my arms to him and invite him in.

He drops to his knees in front of me.

"And that boy is your soul mate?" he asks.

I shake my head. "No. You're my soul mate. I love you."

He takes my hands, turns them over, and presses a kiss to each palm.

"Let me tell you a story."

"Alright," I whisper.

He looks up at me, eyes warm and full of love.

"Once upon a time, there was a boy, who above all else wanted to love and to be loved."

I swallow the lump in my throat and nod. "Good beginning."

"It gets better," he says. "When he was eight, the boy's mom left and although he didn't know it, the next year his life would change forever."

I nod. Will's dad would realize he was a prodigy. He'd lose his childhood. I stroke my thumb across his hand.

"But," he says with a smile, "before that happened, he met a girl and he fell in love."

I think of him pushing me in the mud and I smile. Not the best way to show love.

"He dreamed about that girl, lived for her smile and the moments he caught sight of her. She kept him dreaming, kept him hopeful and believing there might be good in the world. That someday, he might have a friend again. Every time the boy drifted too far into the cold and distant place where he couldn't be reached, she'd come and smile and yank him back into the world."

I squeeze his hands and let him know I understand. He presses another kiss to my palm.

"Then the girl said she was going to marry the boy's

brother. And since the boy had loved the girl for years and would go on loving her for the rest of his life, he decided to stop her."

"Thank goodness," I say.

"Thank goodness," he agrees. "Because I knew from the minute I laid eyes on you, that you and I were meant to be."

My heart feels so happy and so full.

"We made it," he says. "We should be friends."

My breath catches in my throat. "What did you say?"

He nods, and his eyes are a clear chicory blue. "We can take care of each other."

My body tingles as I take in what he's saying. It's not the boy in my memory saying it, it's Will.

"You?" I ask.

The side of his mouth lifts up in a half-smile. Then he opens the drawer of his nightstand and pulls out a leather-bound book. He opens it to the center page and holds it up to me.

It's the chicory flower, dried and faded with time, but there it is—the flower I gave...to him. To Will.

"It was you?"

He sets the book aside and pulls me into his lap on the floor.

All those years I'd thought the boy in the tree was Gavin, and it was Will.

He sets his forehead to mine and looks into my eyes.

"You've loved me from the first," I say. My voice is full of awe.

"And you've always loved me," he says, a smug note in his voice. His lower lip curls into a smile and I think about kissing him.

"But your dad called for Gavin and you ran...I thought...I..." All these years.

It was Gavin who pushed me in the mud. It was Will who was in the tree.

Will quirks an eyebrow. "Whenever my dad called one of us, he expected both of us to come. I never said my name was Gavin."

My cheeks heat. *All these years.* A thought strikes me.

"Erma was right! You're my soul mate."

Will shakes his head. "We were right. We knew it twenty years ago. We just had to figure some things out between then and now."

I smile and rub my hand down his cheek. "Like what?"

"Like what books we love."

I curl into his warm chest. "Mhm."

"And we had to learn how to dance together."

"That's important," I agree. "What else?"

"Whether we like spaghetti, and kissing in the rain."

"We do," I say.

He smiles and takes my lips in a kiss. Then, "And how we like our chocolate."

"Spicy. And blindfolded."

He grins. "And if we like sports or just climbing trees."

"Just trees."

"And where we want to live," he adds.

"Here," I say, and he nods.

"And how many kids we want," he continues. He pulls me closer and trails a line of kisses down my cheek.

"A dozen," I tease.

His eyes light up and I wrap my legs around him.

"And then we have to practice making them. It takes a lot of practice," he says.

He spreads his hands over my lower back and I rock into him.

"Years' worth of practice," I say.

He takes my mouth and sets a kiss full of love against my lips.

"Every day," he agrees.

I send my hands over him and realize how blessed, how wonderfully blessed I am. To love and to be loved.

"I love you," Will whispers fiercely against my mouth.

He rolls back to the floor and pulls me on top of him. I nestle into him and feel his warmth and the beating of his heart.

"I need you to know something," I say. I press my fingers to his cheeks and look into his eyes.

"What is it?"

"I love you. I loved you before I knew you were my soul mate and I loved you when I thought you weren't. And I'm going to keep on loving you, come what may."

He smiles and pulls me close. His lips rub against mine. "Promise?"

I start to laugh. I feel so light. So happy. So loved. "Promise."

He takes my mouth and kisses me with all his love. The love from yesterday, from today, and for tomorrow. For always and forever.

THE END

GET A BONUS EPILOGUE

Want more Jessie and Will? Get an exclusive bonus epilogue for newsletter subscribers only.

When you join the Sarah Ready Newsletter you get access to sneak peaks, insider updates, exclusive bonus scenes and more.

Join Today!

www.sarahready.com/newsletter

ALSO BY SARAH READY

Stand Alone Romances:

The Fall in Love Checklist

Hero Ever After

Soul Mates in Romeo Romance Series:

Chasing Romeo

Love Not at First Sight

Romance by the Book

Find these books and more by Sarah Ready at:

www.sarahready.com/romance-books

Sign up to receive bonus content, exclusive epilogues and more at:
www.sarahready.com/newsletter

ABOUT THE AUTHOR

Author Sarah Ready writes contemporary romance and romantic comedy. Her books have been described as "euphoric", "heartwarming" and "laugh out loud". Her debut novel *The Fall in Love Checklist* was hailed as "the unicorn read of 2020".

Before writing romance full-time Sarah had lots of fun teaching at an Ivy League. Then she realized she could have even more fun writing romance. Her favorite things after writing are adventuring and travel. You'll frequently find her using her degree at a dino dig site, crawling into a cave, snorkeling, or on horseback riding through the jungle – all fodder for her next book. She's lived in Scotland, Norway, Portugal, Switzerland and NYC. She currently lives in the Caribbean with her water-obsessed pup and her awesome family. You can visit her online at www.sarahready.com

Stay up to date, get exclusive epilogues and bonus content. Join Sarah's newsletter at www.sarahready.com/newsletter.